PERSUADING THE DRAGON

Stonefire Dragons #12

JESSIE DONOVAN

Mythical Lake Press, LLC

Persuading the Dragon
Copyright © 2020 Laura Hoak-Kagey
Mythical Lake Press, LLC
First Print Edition

Cover Art by Laura Hoak-Kagey of Mythical Lake Design
ISBN: 978-1944776138

Books in this series:

Persuading the Dragon Synopsis

Nearly a year ago, an injured human female showed up on Stonefire's land carrying a flash drive full of information stolen from the Dragon Knights. However, before Zain Kinsella could interrogate her, she fell into a coma and hasn't awoken since. After his initial anger fades, he wonders if the thin, pale girl will ever wake again. When she does, it's up to him to help guard her and make her strong enough to face some questioning. He most definitely shouldn't notice her delicious heat or the sadness in her eyes. She's a prisoner and can be nothing more.

Ivy Passmore finds herself inside a dragon-shifter hospital, bedridden and barely able to sit up. Despite the overwhelming grief at the death of her brother, she's determined to do everything she can to atone for her part in helping the Dragon Knights and causing her brother's murder. She's more than ready to tell the dragons everything. When one tall, quiet Protector makes a deal—she endures his physical therapy, and he'll help track down her brother's killers—Ivy has no choice but to agree. Slowly, her idea of dragon-shifters changes, especially around one certain dragonman.

As two former enemies morph into something more, the Dragon Knights find out about Ivy's location and offer a reward for her death or capture. Will Stonefire be forced to give her up to protect their clan? Or, will Zain and Ivy be able to find a path where they can defeat the Knights and be together?

The Stonefire and Lochguard series intertwine with one another. Since so many readers ask for the overall reading order, I've included it with this book. (This list is as of May 2020 and you can view the most up-to-date version is available on my website.)

Treasured by the Dragon (Stonefire Dragons #13 / Sept 24, 2020)

Short stories that can be enjoyed any time after *Winning Skyhunter / The Dragon's Discovery*:

Meeting the Humans (Stonefire Dragons Shorts #1)
The Dragon Camp (Stonefire Dragons Shorts #2)
The Dragon Play (Stonefire Dragons Shorts #3)

Semi-related dragon stories set in the USA, beginning sometime around *The Dragon's Discovery / Transforming Snowridge*:

The Dragon's Choice (Tahoe Dragon Mates #1)
The Dragon's Need (Tahoe Dragon Mates #2)
The Dragon's Bidder (Tahoe Dragon Mates #3, July 16, 2020)

Chapter One

I vy Passmore slowly opened her eyes, only to blink them against the bright light above her.

Her mind was foggy, and it took everything she had on getting her eyes to stay open and focus.

Although once she did, the bare, cream walls and white ceiling told her nothing of where she was.

Something about her running through a forest, trying to find dragon-shifters came back to her.

Why would she go looking for dragons? She hated them. She'd heard stories of how they'd terrorized some of her coworkers before. Besides, everyone knew the dragon-shifters would soon demand humans to help increase their numbers, whether the women wanted to go or not. To deny them meant risking their wrath, and really, what chance did a human have of winning against someone who could change into a beast?

After all, a group of dragons flying in the sky could

take over any small town or village in the UK without breaking a sweat.

She tried turning over to her side but couldn't budge an inch. Her entire body was heavy, as if rocks were stacked on top of her chest to keep her from moving.

While Ivy had never been the strongest person in the world, she could bloody turn over. Something was wrong with her.

Trying to make a sound, a barely audible gurgle escaped. Within seconds, a man's face came into view, his dark brows drawn together.

She had no idea who he was, but his brown eyes took in her face, as if he needed to catalogue every detail.

Then he moved better into her view, and she noticed the tattoo on his upper bicep. Her heart skipped a beat and she resisted screaming.

It was a dragon-shifter.

And given how she'd worked with the Dragon Knights, who made it their goal to eradicate dragon-shifters at every opportunity, her chances didn't look good.

He'd probably kill her.

She tried to scream, but only more gurgling escaped. The dragonman sighed before his Northern English accent filled the room. "So you're awake. Now, calm the fuck down already."

Ivy remained still—not that she could move much beyond her eyes and her lips—and waited to see what he'd do.

She was currently helpless. Maybe that could save

her. Dragons were ruthless, but if they had wanted to kill her, they would've done it already, right?

He muttered, "I'll fetch the doctor. Maybe you'll listen to them. However, we're not done yet. You and I are going to see a lot of each other." He leaned an inch closer. "Because you're going to tell me why you showed up here, not to mention what you know of the Knights."

The dragonman leaned back and left before she could even think of how to respond to that.

Although his words niggled at something, a memory at the back of her mind.

Running through the forest, her stomach gnarling with hunger.

Dragons flying in the sky above.

The answer was so close, but just out of reach. If she could growl convincingly, Ivy would've done it right then.

It wasn't as if she had amnesia. She remembered her name and that she lived in Brighton.

She also had a brother, Richard.

The name triggered overwhelming grief. It flooded her body, making her heart squeeze.

Then she remembered: Richard was dead. So was his long-term partner, David.

And it had something to do with her.

Tears prickled her eyes. Damn it, why couldn't she remember everything?

Was her brother's death related to the dragons? If so, it'd give her even more reason to hate the bastards.

And yet, for some reason, she didn't think it had been them. But who else would kill her brother?

Someone entered her room, garnering her attention.

Ivy managed to turn her head a few inches to see the visitor.

A tall woman with mousy brown hair pulled into a ponytail walked toward her, the lab coat and stethoscope around her neck denoting her as a doctor.

When her pupils flashed to slits, Ivy stilled again. Another dragon-shifter.

She was more afraid of the dragon doctor than the muscled dragonman. Instinctively, Ivy knew that someone could cause far more long-lasting pain with drugs and medical science than with a physical beating.

After all, the Dragon Knights had been using drugs as their main focus in the last few years, experimenting on dragons when they could.

Drugs she'd helped formulate.

More information hovered just outside her reach. Had she killed someone related to these dragon-shifters? If that was so, then she had no bloody idea why they'd kept her alive. Weren't they supposed to be bloodthirsty when it came to revenge?

The dragon doctor spoke in the same Northern English accent as the man. "My name is Dr. Sid. And I can see from the terror in your eyes that you're afraid of me. Now, I can only imagine the stories you've heard over the years, ones that made you want to work with the bloody Dragon Knights. However, I uphold the same oath as any human doctor in that I do no harm. I'm part of the reason you're awake right now, and still alive. So I suggest calming down and answering me truthfully. Lies will only hurt you in the long run, and that will be your own damn fault."

Ivy nearly blinked at the dragonwoman's words. Would she truly try to help her if she were honest? Yes, the doctor *had* kept Ivy alive until now. Although she still had no idea for what purpose.

Trust wasn't something she'd give to any dragon-shifter, but if the doctor could help her get better, then Ivy would at least be honest concerning her health.

Because once she had all her memories and fully recovered her strength, she'd need to find some way to escape the dragons and head back to her home down south.

Dr. Sid studied her a second before asking, "Can you talk? Speak if you can, or else blink twice for no."

She tried to say she could, but her throat and mouth were dry, and all that came out was "Aaahhhh."

The dragonwoman reached into one of her pockets, extracted a small plastic bag filled with ice chips, and opened it. "Here, let's try this first."

Dr. Sid placed an ice chip at Ivy's lips. The coolness mixed with wetness made her realize how thirsty she was.

Seeing as the dragons hadn't killed her when unconscious, she parted her lips to accept the ice. As it melted down her throat, she nearly moaned.

After a few more, Dr. Sid stopped and asked, "How about now?"

She croaked, "I think I can."

While her voice was faint and somewhat scratchy to her own ears, it seemed to be enough for the doctor who asked, "Do you hurt anywhere?"

Shaking her head was easier, so Ivy did that. The doctor continued, "Can you wiggle a finger?"

Unsure, Ivy concentrated. She must've succeeded before the dragonwoman nodded. "Good. Now let's try other parts of your body. But don't be alarmed if you can't move much just yet. You've been in a coma for about a year, and your muscles have atrophied. It's going to take some intensive physical therapy to get you walking again, let alone for you to regain the ability to sit upright without help."

Ivy blinked. She'd been out over a year?

Just what the bloody hell had happened to her?

Not that she had much time to think about it. The dragon doctor pushed her to answer questions and try moving various parts of her body. But during the entire set of questions and tests, all Ivy wanted was for her memory to fully return.

It was bad enough she'd lost an entire year of her life —although granted, still being alive at the hands of dragon-shifters was better than dead—but she desperately wanted every memory back she'd possessed before setting foot on the dragons' lands.

Because only then could she really start to piece back together what had happened to her and plan the next steps of her future.

AFTER A FUCKING year of waiting around for the female to wake up, Zain Kinsella hated the fact he had to wait some more.

He paced Dr. Sid's office, anxious for her to return. While it was Zain's job to get as much information out of Ivy Passmore as he could manage, he couldn't begin his task until her health was deemed out of the danger zone.

And given how she'd barely been able to move her head, she could be in that zone for quite a while yet.

His inner dragon spoke up. *It's not as if she's able to run away any time soon considering her health and that the world at large thinks she's dead.*

That's not the point. While Nathan and Lucien have managed to interpret some of the data from the thumb drive we found on her, she could fill in the remaining gaps with passwords and how to break the encrypted files. Maybe then we'd have the information we need to finally defeat the Dragon Knights.

Roughly a year ago, Ivy Passmore had called out for help in the forest near Stonefire. She'd been unconscious by the time Zain had found her. But searching her body had revealed a gold mine—a trove of information about the Dragon Knights, stored on a tiny thumb drive wrapped in plastic. On it had been their formulas, the location of most of their hideouts—both online and physical—as well as some of their recruiting operations and tactics.

But quite a few of the files were strongly encrypted. Not even Stonefire's best IT specialists had been able to break them, to the point that a fair bit of the information was still a mystery.

And to someone like Zain, who liked to act more than sit around and be patient, it was bloody torture waiting for Ivy to recover. The crucial bit of intel they needed to finally eradicate one of Stonefire's main enemies was nearly within their reach; he could feel it.

His dragon grunted. *Be patient. She can't reveal anything if she's dead.*

Zain replied to his beast, *I'm more than aware of her value. It's why she's still alive. But every day that passes is another that could end with a dead or injured dragon-shifter somewhere. Are you okay with that?*

His beast huffed. *Of course not, you idiot. But we're not mind readers. Help her recover her strength, or else we'll get nowhere. If she falls back into another coma, then where will we be?*

Zain didn't know all the medical details, but Stone-fire's main doctors—Sid and Gregor—along with their researchers, Trehan and a human named Emily Davies, had all agreed that the antidote they'd devised to counter the poison and wake Ivy up might not last forever. Only time, testing, and observation would let them know if the change was permanent.

He curled the fingers of one hand into a fist and resisted punching something. *If you think her frail state is going to make me pity her, or become sympathetic, then you're delusional. The Dragon Knights have fucking harmed many of our friends and clan members. They're no better than the dragon hunters, who killed our friend Charlie.*

Charlie Wells had been one of Stonefire's Protectors. She'd been killed a couple of years ago when the dragon hunters had drained her blood to sell on the black market. Since dragon's blood had healing properties for humans, it was incredibly lucrative for criminals.

His dragon growled. *If you continue to let your hatred cloud your judgment, Kai will assign someone else to interrogate her, maybe even himself.*

Kai Sutherland was head Protector of Stonefire, in charge of all clan security, and Zain's boss.

As he debated whether to reply or ignore his dragon —they'd had many arguments about the human female over the last year—Dr. Sid finally walked into the room, with her mate and fellow doctor, Gregor, right behind her.

Zain raised his brows. "Well?"

Sid mirrored his actions. "Your alpha tone isn't helping your case, Zain."

His dragon snorted, but Zain ignored him. Dragon-shifter doctors were a brand of their own, and he knew Sid didn't take anyone's attitude or shit. "Apologies. What did you find out?"

Sid shrugged. "She's awake and remembers most of who she is. Although I can't tell if she's lying about not knowing why she's here, let alone whether she knows she's on Stonefire or not. A combination of waiting and questioning should determine if she's acting or truly has partial amnesia. Although I will say that anything is possible given how that drug knocked her unconscious for nearly a year."

Fucking brilliant. If the human had even partial amnesia, that would make his job that much more difficult. "And how's her health? I need to know when I can talk to her again."

Sid glanced at Gregor, and the mated pair shared a look, one that didn't bode well for him.

Dr. Sid finally answered, "She's incredibly weak, Zain. I can't allow you to question her for some time. She needs to get stronger and then build up muscle strength again. As it is, she barely stayed awake for fifteen minutes before falling back asleep."

Gregor grunted and added in his Scottish accent, "Cassidy's right. There's no point in you hovering around the human, aye? We'll let you know when she's strong enough to face you."

Zain resisted a curse. "Are you banning me from her room? Because even if I can't interrogate her, she could mumble something in her sleep that could help the clan."

Gregor sighed. "So you're going to stay by her side for nearly every minute now? That'll just put you in the way, lad. And if nothing else, it'll make her recovery take longer since she'll be nervous around any dragon-shifter and may not sleep as well as she needs to."

Sid made a noise in agreement. "One of the nurses will be available to the human at all times, and there are also security cameras throughout the building. While we don't usually place cameras in the patient rooms, she's a special case, and I'll allow one. But only if I can turn it off whenever she's naked, or I think she needs some privacy."

He wanted to spit out that dragon-shifters didn't view nudity the same way as humans—you couldn't be modest when you had to be naked to shift into a dragon.

However, he didn't want to piss off Dr. Sid, either. Arguments were the surest way to do that, as he'd learned long ago. So he kept his tone as neutral as he could manage as he said, "If you let me visit her once a day when she's conscious, I promise I won't do anything to endanger her recovery. But even just one question a day could greatly help Nathan and Lucien with the cryptic, unsolved data."

For a beat, neither doctor said anything. Then Gregor finally spoke to his mate, "One question couldn't hurt, Cassidy. Especially if the camera is recording and we can watch to make sure he behaves."

Zain clenched his jaw. He wasn't a new Protector, fresh out of his British Army training like Dacian. He fucking knew how to behave and didn't need to be observed.

His dragon spoke up. *Gregor tries to provoke you all the time on purpose. Stop rising to the bait.*

Stupid Scottish dragons and their ways.

I dare you to say that to his face. Sid will never allow you back into the surgery again, not even if you're missing an arm and are spurting blood from a severed artery.

Not needing to get any more riled up than he already was—which talking with his dragon would most assuredly do—Zain focused back on the doctors, who were having that strange mated-pair conversation with their expressions.

Maybe most wouldn't notice it, but Zain was trained to watch body language. And given how he hated secrets, mated-pair conversations were fucking annoying.

Sid finally looked at Zain again. "Okay, one question a day. That's it. So think carefully about what you're going to ask her beforehand. Because even something like asking, 'What's your favorite color?' will count, Zain Kinsella. Those are my terms."

He grunted, knowing he wouldn't get more from Sid, not even if he pushed for days. "Fine, I agree. And since I haven't asked her any questions today, let me know when she's conscious again."

Sid looked about ready to say something, so Zain turned and exited the room.

As he walked down the familiar corridor that led to the rear exit of the building, he clenched and unclenched his fingers. Kai had refused to give him any other important duties until his current task—finding out everything he could from the human female—was accomplished. Which meant he could either test Dacian's skills to determine if he met the Protectors' standards or wait around for Ivy to wake up.

Needing to shift and spread his wings, he decided on the former.

Although he hoped the young male was well-rested, Zain was a tough trainer and evaluator. And given his shitty day so far, his surliness would only make it that much more challenging for the male.

Chapter Two

Ivy lost count of how many times she drifted in and out of consciousness. The only good thing was that she hadn't fallen back into a permanent coma.

Each time she awoke, bits and pieces of her memory returned. She'd finally remembered why she was with a bunch of dragon-shifters, too—she'd sought them out.

Of course, she had also remembered that her brother had been murdered because of her running away from the Dragon Knights' operation. At first, she'd tried to hide from the Knights with Richard and David, at their house on the outskirts of Brighton. But one day when she'd gone out to buy groceries, someone had gotten to them. She'd found the pair with their throats slit and the symbol of the Knights—a shield with a lance behind it— drawn on the wall in the living room.

She'd never forget that sight for the rest of her life, either. Her brother and brother-in-law had died simply because they'd tried to help her.

Even thinking about it now, tears threatened to fall. She'd loved them both so much. They had been her only family in the world. And in retrospect, she'd been young and foolish to join the Dragon Knights straight out of university. At twenty-one, Ivy hadn't seen how her actions would one day affect those she loved best in the world.

But they had. And it was something she'd have to struggle with for the remainder of life.

If losing Richard and David hadn't been bad enough, she'd only been able to report the murders to the police without giving out specifics of her ties to the Knights to catch the killers—which they would never do, anyway. The Dragon Knights were exceedingly careful and even had moles in the various police departments. One whisper of what she'd been, and she'd be as good as dead.

So at the first opportunity, she'd resorted to her last option: to run to the dragon-shifters and give them the information she'd stolen from the Knights' database. True, she'd hated and feared dragons for most of her life, but if there was anyone who could—and would—take revenge on the Knights, it was the dragon-shifters.

Enemy of an enemy was a friend, and all that.

What she hadn't counted on was passing out on Stonefire's land and then falling into a coma for a year. The doctors still hadn't told her why it'd happened, or if it could happen again.

Which meant her time could be short, and she needed to convince them to listen to her. Without her knowledge, they'd never crack all the information on the thumb drive and truly be able to take down the Knights.

However, no one smiled at her or even tried to initiate a conversation that didn't revolve around her health. To get them to listen to anything she said, and believe it, was going to take some work.

One of the doctors—Dr. Lewis, a dragonman with dark hair and glasses who spoke with a Welsh accent— walked into the room. Out of the three doctors she'd encountered so far, Ivy preferred him the most. He rarely spoke unless necessary, and he never lingered after completing his routine checks on her health. He oddly didn't view her with malice, or any emotion, really, beyond curiosity.

Maybe he was the one who would believe she had information the dragons still needed.

After checking her vital signs on the machines, he asked, "Any noticeable changes?"

"No. I'm still always tired and weak."

Half-truth. She'd recovered all of her memory, but she wasn't going to share that just yet.

He scribbled down something on his clipboard. "Then tomorrow you'll start some light physical therapy. However, if anything hurts before then or during the process, make sure to say something."

She'd barely nodded before he left the room.

So much for swaying Dr. Lewis to her side. Maybe he was too aloof for her purposes.

Not that she had time to do more than notice he'd left because a second later, the dragonman with dark hair and eyes, the one she'd first seen upon waking, strode into the room.

He pulled up a stool next to her bed, sat down, and

crossed his arms over his chest.

No doubt he tried to intimidate her with his bulging muscles and much bigger form. But given how much effort the doctors were investing to save her, he wouldn't dare hurt her.

At least not yet.

The dragonman stared, and she stared back. If dragon-shifters weren't much more than animals, which a lot of people believed, then she couldn't show her fear, or he'd pounce.

Although in the back of her mind, Ivy started to think dragon-shifters were more human than animal. But she quickly rejected it. If she accepted they were a lot like her, it would invalidate a good chunk of her life.

Focus on your endgame, Ivy. That's all that matters.

Right, the destruction of the Dragon Knights.

Wanting the dragonman to leave her alone so she could work on a plan, she croaked, "What do you want?"

He remained silent. And as the seconds ticked by, Ivy hated how she couldn't even sit up in bed, let alone turn over to give him her back and dismiss him.

However, there was one thing she could do. And even though she shouldn't irritate the dragonman, she closed her eyes to feign sleep.

He grunted. "Don't even think of going to sleep until I'm done with you."

Her eyes flew open. His brusque tone ruffled her feathers. "I'm tired, so go away."

He raised his brows. "You were in a coma for a year. If I were in your shoes, then I'd want to try and stay awake as long as possible."

Normally, if she were at her full strength, Ivy would argue back. Standing up for herself was how she'd soared up the ranks of the Dragon Knights, until she'd become the head of an entire research department.

But every inch of her body ached, and it was true— she was exhausted. So she merely murmured, "I'm going to close my eyes in two minutes and go to sleep. So if you have something to say, do it before then."

His pupils flashed to slits and back, and Ivy was glad she couldn't jump or really even flinch. Even though she'd watched videos during her early days with the Knights and knew it meant a dragon-shifter was talking with their inner beast, it also reminded her of the monster within. One who could come out and wreak havoc on any person they wanted.

Sure, the Department of Dragon Affairs—or DDA —claimed to have everything under control, but it wasn't the full truth. Ivy had seen the damage done in some of the more remote areas of the UK, not to mention other parts of Europe. Some dragons took what they wanted, escaped, and were never caught or later punished.

Because, really, how would a government agency take down a full-sized dragon without using an illegal weapon or chemical agent?

The man finally spoke again. "What was your role inside the Dragon Knights?"

Ivy struggled to keep her eyes open. Even if this was the golden opportunity to convince him they needed her help with decoding the encrypted data, she couldn't stay awake much longer. Maybe if she gave him a hint, he'd come back later, when she had more energy. So she murmured, "I was a researcher."

He opened his mouth to say something, but Dr. Sid came in and pushed the man away until he stood and moved. She said, "That's enough, Zain. I have a few more things to check before Ivy falls asleep again."

Even though the dragonwoman was shorter and less muscled than the man, he merely gave a curt nod and left the room.

Zain was his name, apparently.

Dr. Sid moved closer to her bed and said, "If he bothers you too much, then let me know, and I'll keep him away."

Ivy wondered why Dr. Sid would care. Sure, they wanted her alive for some unknown reason. Although after Zain's question, she suspected they wanted all the information on her research and projects from her time with the Knights.

Still, there was no reason for the female doctor to be even tangentially nice to her for the first time.

Especially since dragon-shifters weren't supposed to care about humans, beyond their ability to give them babies.

Dr. Sid raised an eyebrow. "Okay, then, don't answer. But for the moment, I'm on your team, Ivy. Don't give me a reason to switch sides."

Her eyelids drooped, but she blinked them open again. Before she could think better of it, she blurted, "Why?"

"Because I've looked at some of the recruitment videos and tactics, and I can see how they could influence someone. They're completely bullshit, but convincing. And if you can be persuaded to the truth, then maybe others could, too." Ivy opened her mouth, but Dr. Sid continued before she could say a word. "Right then, it's time for you to get some more rest. Tomorrow you're going to have someone move your limbs and get them used to a little movement. And it could bloody well hurt after so long of disuse. So, rest and conserve your energy."

Something about the dragonwoman's tone of voice made Ivy want to listen to her. It was strange since she'd never really experienced the feeling before, the desire to obey.

Maybe dragon-shifters did have some strange magic of their own.

However, she gave up the fight to keep her eyes open and drifted off into a dreamless sleep.

ZAIN SAT WITH HIS BOSS, Kai Sutherland, along with the two IT specialists who had been working on cracking Ivy's thumb drive data. He was more familiar with Nathan, who worked specifically with the Protectors. However, over the last year, Zain had come to value Lucien's input as well, even if he sometimes would unconsciously switch to his second language of French when he was working on a problem.

But given the male's mother was French, it at least somewhat made sense.

Kai finally spoke for the first time after Zain had

revealed Ivy's role. "If she was a researcher, then she's more valuable than we thought. Everything needs to be done to help her recover and maybe work on her reversing her brainwashing, too, so that she'll talk to Nathan and Lucien. Shots of dragon-shifter blood should help speed up her recovery time as well, regarding her physical strength."

Zain grunted. "I agree, but anything medically related is in Dr. Sid's hands."

"Maybe," Kai stated. "Right now, Stonefire lacks a physical therapist, and Lochguard is busy using theirs with some injury I don't know the details of. Which means you're going to have to step up and help, Zain."

He frowned. "Yes, I helped with PT whilst in the army, learning all that I could on the job, but I haven't done any of that stuff for years."

Kai shrugged. "Regardless, you're our best chance. And before you mention the doctors again, I'll talk to Sid. She'll say yes. The trick will be in finding a volunteer to give her their blood on a regular basis."

Good luck, Zain thought. Few would want to help a human who had been hell-bent on eradicating their kind.

Zain raised his brows. "You sound pretty confident about Sid."

Kai replied, "She wants my mate's help with something to do with her dragon doctor alliance project. And whilst Jane would do it anyway, I may use it as leverage."

Kai's mate was a former human reporter named Jane Hartley, who had no problem matching Kai's alpha personality. He snorted. "Right, because that'll go down well with Jane."

Kai grunted. "My mate owes me a favor or two. So I'll collect."

Granted, Zain didn't know the first thing about having a mate, let alone a human one. However, he didn't think trading favors was the ideal situation.

Still, if Kai said it would work, Zain believed him. He replied, "I may have some PT training, but I know nothing about deprogramming someone who's been brainwashed. Who's going to help with that?"

Kai didn't miss a beat. "Serafina Rossi. She arrived on Stonefire last week. She worked as a psychologist back in Italy, and she should be able to handle the exit counseling side of things."

"I know she's Brenna's cousin, but how do you know we can trust her?" Zain asked.

Brenna Rossi had been one of Stonefire's Protectors before mating an Irish dragonman and moving there. Zain wished she was still around to help with Ivy. Brenna would've been much better at a fake friendly relationship than Zain ever would.

Lucien spoke up for the first time. "Trust me, I did the most thorough background check I could manage. Serafina was being told what to do with all the clan members, regardless if it was the best for their health or not, by the Italian clan leader. She came here for freedom and the ability to do her job without interference."

Zain frowned. "How the bloody hell did you get that from a background check? Did you call people up and interrogate them?"

Lucien rolled his eyes. "Of course not. But her uncle lives here, and he told us quite a bit. Hacking her emails and personal accounts confirmed most of what Gabriele Rossi told us anyway."

"Should you be hacking so casually, Lucien?" Zain drawled.

The male grinned, his teeth white against his light brown skin. "It's only a problem if you get caught. I'll never get caught."

He was about to say more, but Kai jumped in. "Lucien had permission, end of story. You and Serafina will be working together on this. Once Ivy is in a better place and is strong enough, Lucien and Nathan will join in, too. I don't doubt your interrogation skills—you've done a bloody good job watching over her and getting straight answers so soon—but Lucien and Nathan can probably speak to her in a less intimidating way."

He eyed the two males—one with pale skin and blond hair, the other with light brown skin and black hair, both as muscled as any dragon-shifter in their prime—and snorted. "Right, because they're so much less intimidating."

Nathan cleared his throat. "I don't growl nearly as much as you do, Zain. So that works in my favor."

Lucien chuckled, and Zain glared at one male and then the other. "You two have become way too familiar around me. At one time, neither of you would look me in the eye."

Lucien shrugged—an annoying habit of his—and said, "It's hard to be nervous around someone you've seen singing drunken karaoke."

"It was the one time, and only the one time," Zain bit out.

Kai grunted—his way of snapping them to order—and spoke up only once all eyes were back on him. "Enough bickering, children. We have a general plan, and we'll continue to fine-tune it as we learn more about the human female." Kai looked directly at Zain. "You'll meet with Serafina this afternoon and learn what she needs from you."

He nodded. Kai dismissed Lucien and Nathan. Only once they were alone again did he add, "And play nice with the human. I know she's done horrible things and could even have played a part in attacking Sid or even my sister with those bloody drugs. However, if she can bring down the whole organization, anything is worth achieving that goal."

"Anything?"

"Yes."

Zain wanted to argue, but held back. Kai was the most stubborn bastard he knew, even more so than Stonefire's clan leader at times.

Add in Kai willing to overlook how the Dragon Knights had drugged his sister, making her dragon silent for months, and it told Zain volumes about how important Ivy was to Kai's future plans.

Zain's inner dragon finally spoke up. *Just pretend this is a sort of undercover operation. Play the part of a nice male, maybe the opposite of your usual surliness.*

I'm only surly because I've been relegated to babysitting duty for the last fucking year.

Only because of Ivy Passmore. Get everything we need from her, bring down the Dragon Knights, and maybe Kai will let us do what we really want—to take down the dragon hunters.

More than anything, Zain wanted to avenge his former friend's death. *Fine, I'll be nice. But only so we can take out the bastards who killed Charlie and finally give her mate and son some peace.*

Kai's voice prevented his dragon from replying. "I'll text you the time for the meeting with Serafina. You'll need to bring her up-to-date on Ivy and everything we know about her."

"Fine." Zain stood. "That just means someone else will have to put Dacian through his trials for the afternoon."

"No worries. It's about time I judged his abilities for myself."

Zain didn't envy the younger male at all. If Dacian thought Zain was a tough bastard, then he'd end up in a weakened puddle after Kai's routines.

However, if the younger male couldn't last through them, then he didn't deserve to become a Protector.

With a final bob of his head, Zain exited the room and headed to the office he'd been using to gather and store information on Ivy. Maybe all the prep work he'd done would help him finish the task sooner. Because it'd been far too long since Zain had led a team to root out some dragon hunters. Or he might be able to search for the rogue dragon-shifters who lived in the remote parts of the UK, ones who could destroy all the goodwill and progress the UK dragon clans had made over the last few years with one bad act.

Soon. It wouldn't be long before Zain could forget he'd ever met Ivy Passmore and finally move on with his life.

Chapter Three

The next day, Zain sat in front of a laptop with Serafina Rossi at his side, and asked her, "Are you ready?"

The Italian female was in her early thirties, with long black hair and brown eyes. While she wasn't as straightforward as her cousin Brenna and only talked when absolutely required to do so, Zain couldn't blame her. Reading her file, he'd learned how her entire existence in Italy had been dictated by her former leader.

To be honest, he wasn't sure how she'd secured a transfer to Stonefire. They had become rare between the UK and other mainland European countries in recent years.

His dragon spoke up. *It probably happened because of Bram and Evie moving mountains to get her here, to help Gabriele after losing his mate.*

Since Bram was clan leader and his mate was a

former DDA employee with plenty of connections, his beast was probably right.

Serafina nodded, bringing him out of his head. In perfect English, she said, "Go ahead. I'm ready."

Zain pushed the Play button, sat back, and crossed his arms over his chest.

Even though he'd seen this video a half-dozen times, it still made him uneasy, not to mention full of anger at all the lies.

A distant shot of a burned-out village came onto the screen before panning to a short street with cottages and a small church on fire, smoke billowing up into the air.

Human bodies lay strewn on the street, unmoving. Zain would bet his right arm they were actors. Even so, the blood and open, staring eyes were eerie to the point he nearly shivered.

A voiceover played as the footage continued to zoom in on the destruction. "*This is a tiny village in Yorkshire, one that no one has ever heard of. In the end, not even their small numbers or relative anonymity could save them.*"

The shot switched to the now-smoldering interior of a cottage, a half-burned crib in the corner. The voiceover continued, "*Not even the children were spared.*"

A tiny coffin flashed on the screen, lying next to several more rows of them, switching to what looked to be a former classroom, the chairs and desks mostly warped metal and melted plastic. "*But did the dragon-shifters, who claim they treasure children, care? No. They wanted this land for their own, to steal the food and livestock from the nearby farms. Even if the villagers would've stayed away like any sane person would, the dragons wouldn't hear of it.*"

"And we know this because of a survivor."

The image changed to a silhouette of a woman. Distorted sniffles played before her altered voice came on. *"I-I begged them to stop, to spare my baby."* More sniffles. *"B-But they laughed, handed her to one of them in their dragon form, and I had to sit and watch helpless as they took her into the air and dropped her not ten feet away from me. M-My poor baby."*

She broke down into sobs, putting her face into her hands.

One of the tiny coffins came back onto the screen again, along with the voiceover. *"This is the true nature of the dragon-shifters. The media and the DDA give you happy stories and try to convince you that the dragons won't hurt us. But they do that for only one reason—to save their jobs. Nothing else matters. And as we know, the dragons only want our land, our women, and even our lives. They're monsters."*

Line after line of graves rolled by, until it stopped at one not yet filled in, a tiny coffin being lowered into the ground.

The voiceover continued, *"Don't let this happen to you or your family. The dragons must be killed, every last one of them. Join our cause today and make it happen before it's too late, and we lose the war. Because if we do lose, then all of England is doomed."*

The mushroom cloud of an atomic bomb appeared before a web address flashed a few times.

The video stopped, and Zain glanced at Serafina. "This is one of hundreds we managed to download from the thumb drive we retrieved."

She kept her gaze on the screen. "I need to watch all of them then. But what of the website they advertised?"

He grunted. "It's a dead end. It redirected more than a dozen times and bounced off so many servers that our specialists couldn't track it. They change the address in each video, and our best guess is that they only let it work for a short period before disabling it."

Serafina finally met his gaze, her eyes neutral, not betraying a single thought. "There's one other piece of information that would be helpful to have so I can treat the human. Do you know who the leader of the Dragon Knights is? Because if not, that's one of the things I'd like you to try to find out. Knowing about the hierarchy will make it easier for me to talk with the female."

Under the table, Zain clenched his fingers into a fist. "No, we don't know who's in charge. We're not even sure if there's a single leader or just an anonymous online persona who acts like it."

"Well, at least try to find out more while I go through the data and watch all videos."

He frowned. "So when will you talk with Ivy?"

"Soon, but not quite yet. It'll be easier if I have all the information to craft the best treatment plan, although no dragon-shifter has had to deal with a former Dragon Knight like this—at least, there's no record of it—so it's going to be a sort of ad hoc approach. Anyone who talks with her needs to note any change in her behavior or even her beliefs about us, and report it to me."

Zain decided the psychologist needed to know one more thing before he left. "We have a camera in her room. The doctors turn it off when the human needs privacy, but otherwise, you can watch it any time, if that will help."

Serafina bobbed her head. "Yes, that will be quite helpful. Once I finish watching all the propaganda videos, then I'll observe her to decide the next moves. For all we know, talking with others may be all that she needs in the beginning."

He frowned. "She won't be talking with you? I thought that's why you came here, to help her?"

She raised an eyebrow. "I'll be doing plenty. Once Ivy begins to accept reality over lies like those in the video we watched, she'll struggle internally. Not to mention that according to the notes in her file you gave me, there's the grief with her brother. I need to decide when to talk with her—not too soon or too late. On top of that, her entire reality is about to be destroyed. I'd rather she not lash out at me in the early days, or she may never trust me to help her in the long run."

He resisted growling because it sounded like a whole lot of nothing to Zain.

His dragon spoke up. *She has the training. We should trust her.*

It all seems wishy-washy to me.

Serafina's voice prevented his beast from replying. "I know dragon-shifters prefer action over waiting in most cases. It's only natural, given our inner beasts. However, I want what's best for Ivy. Not only because she's my patient now, and it's my duty, but this is a test for me, too. I won't screw up and be sent back to Italy if I can help it."

The determination in her words made both man and beast take notice. Zain would bet everything he had that the female would rather cut off her own hand than go back to her old clan. "I'll try to be understanding, but you'll probably have to keep explaining things to me."

The female smiled for the first time, making her look younger. "I can do that. No one ever asked me to explain anything back on Clan LupoForesta. So ask me a question any time, and I'll do my best."

His natural curiosity wanted to know more, but Zain had his hands full with Ivy. So he restrained himself from asking more about Serafina's past. "Right, then I won't hesitate to ask questions when I have them." He motioned toward the laptop. "Go ahead and watch as many as you can stomach. I'll check in on you later, but Lucien and Nate are also available if I can't answer you right away."

The female bobbed her head and immediately turned on the next video. He had a feeling she'd watch as many as she could without any sort of break, unlike him and the others who'd hadn't been able to stomach more than a few before storming out. Zain said to his dragon, *I wonder if she's always so focused.*

Remember this is probably the first time she's been able to do her job without someone telling her how to treat someone. Yes, she doesn't want to go back to her old clan. But she most likely feels useful again for the first time in ages.

I guess you're right. Maybe we'll be useful again soon, too.

As he made his way out of the Protectors' main building, Zain switched his focus from the psychologist to his upcoming task with Ivy.

In order to help Serafina, he'd have to use his limited amount of question time to try and figure out if *(a)* Ivy had ever met the leader of the Knights, and (*b*) if he or she even existed or was just an anonymous persona.

Since he wouldn't be able to do either until she was awake and rested enough, Zain headed back to his cottage. He'd scan her files again—he kept a copy at home in addition to his office—just in case he'd missed something. While Stonefire's Protectors had uncovered early on in their background check on Ivy about her brother's murder, he'd rather not bring it up until she was stronger.

However, if she refused to cooperate and tell him what he wanted, then he'd do whatever was necessary to move his mission forward.

Chapter Four

Ivy missed the days of being able to eat or drink on her own.

The glass of water sat on a table next to her bed, but she didn't have enough energy to reach out and pick it up. And even if she could, holding it up and guiding the straw to her mouth was beyond her capabilities.

Ivy had never been a physically fit person to begin with, but certainly she could pick up a bloody glass when she wanted.

Staring at it, she debated calling for one of the nurses. Usually the stony-faced, determined nurse named Ginny answered her call. However, Ivy wasn't sure if she had the energy to deal with her. The dragonwoman demanded a clear request, complete with please and thank you, before she did anything.

And even then, she'd give a glare before proceeding.

The only clue Ivy had about the woman's animosity

was a one-time mutter: *"She could've been the one to hurt Sid, and now we're helping her."*

Not that Ivy could ask Ginny about what had been done to Dr. Sid. As it was, the nurse said the bare minimum. Divulging secrets was most definitely not part of her job.

Before Ivy could weigh the severity of her thirst against facing the nurse, the door opened, and the dragon-shifter named Zain walked in.

Since this was the first time she could get a good look at him without confusion or exhaustion, she noticed he was tall, as all dragons were, with dark hair and eyes. His skin was slightly tanned, which was strange considering it was early summer, and that rarely meant lots of sunshine in the North of England.

His pinched eyebrows and firmly set jaw made the dragonman a little menacing, but now that Ivy was fully aware he couldn't hurt her—not to mention Sid said to call out for her if he made her feel uncomfortable—she wasn't as afraid of him.

However, Ivy wasn't completely immune to the fact he was part dragon, and she itched to get away from him in case he lashed out. At least her heart rate hadn't skyrocketed yet, which was progress.

Same as his last visit, he pulled up a stool and sat near her bed, his arms crossed over his chest and his gaze piercing.

Words slipped out before she could stop them. "What do you want?"

He grunted. "Your voice sounds better. That means

you should be able to give me more thorough answers compared to before."

Of course he wanted information from her—why else would they keep her alive?—but she could use that to her advantage. He was her best chance at getting the dragon-shifters to listen. Only then would they go after her enemies at full force. She bit out, "Answers to what? You don't need to play games. Just ask, and I'll tell you almost anything."

He didn't miss a beat. "Who is the leader of the Dragon Knights?"

Of all the things for him to ask, he'd ask that one. She sighed. "I don't know."

He studied her. "How is that possible?"

The door opened, but Ivy answered while she still could. "Only the inner-most circle had access to the leader. There's a structure in place to minimize the risk of exposure."

Dr. Gregor Innes strode to the other side of her bed. "Are you tired, Ivy?"

She never took her gaze from Zain's and ignored the doctor's question. "Want proof that I'm being sincere? One of the passwords is FX34KT982. Find the files it'll work on, and they will reveal the structures I mentioned, plus a few more extras that should convince you to listen to me."

She barely noticed Dr. Innes next to her. No, she wanted Zain to take her information and at least try to access the data she wanted him to find. She stared as if her life depended on it, willing him to try out the password straight away.

He stood. "I will. But not before we move your limbs a little. Are you ready?"

She blinked. "Wait, what? I wouldn't have pinned you as a physical therapist."

"I've had enough training to massage and move your limbs a little, so you'll have to deal with me for today."

Dr. Innes grunted, garnering Ivy's attention. "Irritating her isn't part of the plan, Zain."

Zain never took his gaze from her face. "I'm sure she wants to get better as soon as possible, right, human?"

She focused back on Zain. "Yes, but—"

"Good. Then unless you're in extreme pain or need the doctor to look over you right now, let's get started."

As the dragonman stared at her, his pupils flashing between round and slitted, Ivy couldn't look away.

He clearly didn't like her, yet he wanted to get her well as quickly as possible.

Which aligned with her own plans.

So she replied, "I'll be fine, Dr. Innes. I'm ready for whatever Zain has planned."

The Scottish doctor muttered something Ivy couldn't make out, but Zain must have because he narrowed his eyes.

But within a few beats, Ivy was alone with Zain again. She said, "Just try not to break my bones. I know how much you lot like that."

She mentally cursed herself. Angering the dragonman wasn't the best idea.

"Then don't give me a reason to," he stated.

Zain tossed back her blanket, exposing her legs. The cool air made her shiver.

He took one of her bare feet between his hands. His warm, slightly rough fingers sent a rush of heat through her body.

For a second, she froze. *No, no, no.* She couldn't be attracted to a dragon-shifter.

All they wanted women for was to have lots of babies and either kill them in the process or toss them aside when they were too tired to do it anymore.

But as he rubbed her feet—probably to get her circulation going—she barely bit back a gasp at the sparks rushing up her leg.

For a monster who liked to kill for fun, his warm fingers were like magic.

Gritting her teeth, Ivy remembered every video she'd seen of the dragon-caused destruction, every site she'd visited to view the aftermath, and soon controlled her reaction to the dragon-shifter's touch.

It'd been so long since she'd had any skin-to-skin contact that her body would react to an eighty-year-old man.

Yes, that's right. It wasn't because of the dragonman at her feet specifically.

Which she repeated over and over again to herself as he massaged one foot and calf before the other, not caring if it were the truth or not. She couldn't be vulnerable to a dragon's charms, not if she wanted to find a way to escape once she was strong enough to do so.

THE INSTANT IVY'S pupils dilated at his touch, it took everything Zain had to not drop her foot and storm out.

Many human females lusted after dragon-shifters. That wasn't new.

However, she'd dedicated a number of years to eradicate his kind. She couldn't have it both ways.

His dragon spoke up. *If you put her past with the Dragon Knights aside and simply look at her as a female, she's pretty.*

What the fuck are you talking about?

His beast grunted. *I'm merely being honest. I wouldn't notice her ginger hair or blue eyes if you'd take a partner and have sex more often.*

I've been busy, as you well know, watching over the human.

Well, if you want someone we can fuck and discard, she's perfect. After all, once we get the information from her, she'll be handed over to the DDA, and we'll never see her again.

I'm not going to use and discard her, dragon. She's one of our enemies, for fuck's sake. We could be cock-deep inside her and she'd stab us in the back.

His beast snorted. *She can't even sit up by herself, so when would she go find a knife and bring it back here? Not to mention the cameras would alert everyone if she tried it.*

Right, you're spending far too much time thinking about this.

That's not my fault. You're the one who came up with all the stupid rules about which females we could fuck and which we couldn't. Loosen your bloody rules, find a willing partner, and then we wouldn't have this problem.

Yes, Zain had rules. But those rules allowed him to do his job, keep his distance, and prevent a repeat of the disaster he'd had during his time with the British Army almost ten years ago when his superior had tried to coerce him to have sex or be booted out. *Once we finish this assignment, I'll find a willing female. Just don't wax on about this one. She has blood on her hands. Remember that.*

Maybe not literally, but some of the children the Knights had pumped full of drugs—drugs she probably had a hand in—might never get their inner dragons back.

And for a dragon-shifter, that was the equivalent of losing half your soul.

His beast huffed. *We don't know the full extent of her involvement yet, just that she was a researcher. Find out the truth and then pass judgment, not before.*

Don't wish for rainbows and happy endings, dragon. She's our enemy. A useful one, but still an enemy.

Zain finished massaging Ivy's legs and moved up to her right arm.

Staring down at it for a second, he truly noticed how thin and pale she was for the first time.

If he squeezed too hard, she'd probably snap.

No. He wasn't going to feel pity for the human. His clan had already saved her life from the poison in her body, a mixture of chemicals the Knights had been secretly giving her the whole time. Only once she hadn't received the daily antidote had her systems started breaking down, or so the doctors had told him.

How the bloody hell had she missed what they'd been doing to her?

His dragon grunted. *I'd suggest something, but you want to hate her unequivocally, so finish your job. Wake me if we need to shift.*

His beast curled into a ball in the back of his mind and went to sleep.

Aware that he was standing and merely staring at her thin bicep, Zain took her hand in his to begin working his way up the limb.

His hands dwarfed hers. And yet, her tiny hands had probably hurt members of his clan.

The human asked, "What are you staring at? If my cuticles offend you, then don't look."

He narrowed his eyes. "Are you trying to piss me off? Because it wouldn't take much for me to break a finger."

As soon as the words left his lips, he regretted them. He shouldn't encourage her untrue beliefs about his kind.

Ivy raised her brows. "I know how much it must be killing you to hold back and play nice. I'm sure you'll get a new victim to torture or kill soon enough."

Zain should let it go. She was merely trying to rile him up, maybe to figure out some of his weaknesses.

Or, she was just bloody delusional, and nothing he'd say would change her mind anyway.

However, he couldn't help but blurt, "The only one hurting innocents is your former friends, the Knights, as well as the fucking dragon hunters. Who targets children? Oh, you and your kind. You're the monster, not me."

She opened her mouth but closed it. Zain focused on his massage for a few minutes—working his way up her wrist, her forearm, and eventually her bicep—and was about to go to her other arm when her voice filled the room again. "The targeting of children is why I left."

His gaze shot to hers. "What?"

She didn't look away from his eyes. He wasn't sure if he was impressed or annoyed that she kept them free of emotion. "I didn't mind silencing inner dragons. I thought that might help the children lead normal lives. But I had no idea about some of the brutal experiments and torture. Once I discovered that was happening, I knew I had to leave. And since anyone who challenged the decisions made by the higher-ups—unless it was to further hurt dragon-shifters—ended up mysteriously missing, I escaped the Knights and went to hide with my brother."

He had to remind himself not to give her any information about his kind, so Zain didn't mention how losing an inner dragon was nearly as bad as torture for some individuals. "So you only approved certain levels of bigotry and villainy. Good to know."

"You act all self-righteous, but I've seen some of the women down south who were purposely impregnated. And afterward, the dragons stole their babies before tossing the women aside, no matter if they wanted to stay with their children or not. How do you explain that?"

Zain had never heard of those rumors. True, Clan Skyhunter down south had only recently acquired some decent clan co-leaders. Before them, a bastard who'd ended up burying murdered humans on his land had ruled.

It was entirely possible that Marcus King, the former Skyhunter leader, had done as Ivy said. He'd have to ask the other clan about it later.

However, rather than argue, Zain decided to deflect. "I can only speak for my clan, and we never terrorize or hurt humans unless they attack or seek to harm us first."

She paused a second before asking, "What about those villages in Yorkshire and Cumbria? Let me guess—you didn't burn them down or kill babies for sport? Some other creature did it? Ghosts, perhaps? Or demons?"

Ivy was talking about the damn propaganda videos. "First, there aren't any bloody demons or ghosts. And second, everything in those videos was faked. And before you say of course I'd plead innocent, why were the place names never mentioned? Even a little-known village has a name. No, it's always some nameless place in the middle of fucking nowhere. How convenient."

The human opened her mouth and promptly closed it. Thinking she would shut up for a bit, he finished massaging her arms and moved back to her legs.

However, before he could explain what he intended to do next, Ivy blurted, "But how could everything burn so fast? It was hellish dragon fire that left everything so mangled."

He snorted. "For someone supposedly so clever, you can be bloody stupid. Dragon-shifters can't breathe fire. It's get-to-know-a-dragon-shifter 101."

She narrowed her eyes. "You're lying."

He raised his brows. "Am I? Do you want me to bring some of the others in here and show them how thick you are? Because I'll gladly do it. To be honest, it would make my day."

She growled. "You're an arsehole."

He tilted his head. "Says the female who thought it was okay to pump our children full of drugs."

A machine attached to Ivy beeped a few times, and Zain tried to figure out which one. He hadn't intended to rile up the human. But he hadn't been able to help himself.

Dr. Trahern Lewis walked in, glanced at the machines, and pushed Zain back. "Leave. You're putting her health in danger."

Zain looked past the doctor, straight at Ivy. "If you want to confirm the truth, ask Trahern about the fire. You seem to like him best, after all."

He turned and walked out of the room before the human could say anything else.

As he quickly headed toward the exit so he could avoid a scolding from Dr. Sid, he started analyzing what Ivy had shared.

Could it really be true that members of the Dragon Knights thought dragon-shifters breathed fire and burned people alive for entertainment?

His dragon finally woke up. *I wish we could breathe fire.*

I don't. It's one less thing the DDA can restrict, not to mention one less thing for the humans to fear about us.

Still, her words are just further proof of how the Dragon Knights mess with the minds of their recruits. More than us, she needs Serafina's help.

Serafina's still doing some research. Besides, we didn't get the name of the leader, not that Ivy seemed to know it. She just gave us some bloody password to pass on to the others.

Which we need to do as soon as possible. There could be something important behind that protected data.

He grunted his consensus. The human may be his enemy, but any shot at gathering more information on the Knights was one he'd take.

Zain's inner beast continued, *And just think, maybe once*

reality starts filtering in, Ivy will realize the pain she's inflicted on others. She'll definitely do whatever she can to help Stonefire then, even more so than she already has. And then we would finally have the upper hand and could fight and defeat one of our greatest enemies.

No doubt his dragon wanted Ivy to think of them as some kind of hero in the end, just to get some pussy. *The only reason I want her to wake up from the fog of lies is so she can become Lucien and Nathan's problem.*

Until she can walk and function again, she'll be our problem.

Don't remind me.

Zain picked up his pace. He'd give Lucien and Nathan the password she mentioned and then report everything to Serafina. With any luck, the new password would open all of the cryptic data in time. And maybe, just maybe, if that became true, Zain could perform her physical therapy without saying another word.

Because if she continued to get under his skin, he could seriously fuck up his mission by sharing something he shouldn't. And since being a Protector was everything to him, he couldn't allow that to happen.

Then an idea came to him. If Zain taught the most basic of moves to one of the nurses, he wouldn't have to see the human that often. True, he'd have to come back when she reached a certain threshold, but not before.

Yes, that would work. Right after he visited Lucien and Nate, he'd approach Gregor with the idea. Because Zain only wanted to ask the human questions, nothing more. And he may have just figured out how to do that.

Chapter Five

Ivy stared at the door of her room long past after Dr. Lewis had left.

His answer to her question about dragon fire ran on repeat inside her head: *"No, dragons can't breathe fire. It's physically impossible. Let me explain every reason why."*

His scientific jargon had been lost on her, but the fact he had such a detailed explanation made Ivy wonder if she was wrong.

Maybe dragons didn't breathe fire.

And if that was the case, then what elsc had she been taught that was also a lie?

Turning her head against the pillow, Ivy stared at the wall and tried to think of where she'd first learned of dragon fire.

Hadn't it been in elementary school? Or, had it been university?

Somewhere before the Dragon Knights, for sure.

Then it hit her—it'd been during the introductory

counseling sessions she'd done with the Dragon Knights' recruiter.

At the time, she hadn't known the truth behind the organization that called themselves the Friends of the World. They'd had a tent in the city center, offering free therapists and a collection of books about the dragon-shifters. The books had claimed to reveal all the dragon-shifters' secrets.

Ivy had always been afraid of dragons growing up and had purposefully kept her distance. If she stayed out of their way, they'd stay out of hers. But for some reason, she'd gone inside the tent that day. Maybe it had been the attractive man smiling at her, or something he'd said to make her laugh. Either way, she couldn't remember any longer. She'd only been twenty-one years old and had still been searching for who she was.

Back then, Ivy had probably thought the therapists would help her figure it all out.

Regardless, she'd gone home with a few books and a shot of self-confidence.

Only after she'd later read one of the books titled, *The Truth Behind the Dragons of the UK,* had her confidence faded and her smile turned into a gasp of horror.

They'd been so many gruesome stories, with so many deaths and innocent lives stolen.

Many of the victims had been dropped from a great height for fun, almost like a competition among the dragon-shifters.

Not to mention the dragon fire they used for torture, and how survivors had said the dragons had laughed at their screams as they burned alive.

By all rights, the British government should've imprisoned most of the dragons, or sent them to any of the prison colonies around the world designed to hold dragon-shifters.

However, World War II had decimated the dragons' numbers, to the point their population became dangerously low. That's when they'd pretended to be nice to humans again, forming alliances and agreements—dragon's blood in exchange for human females. They'd struck even more bargains with the DDA in the 1980s to counteract the AIDS epidemic.

But as Ivy lay in her hospital bed, one nestled inside a dragon clan, she began to wonder if the books had been written to make her hate them.

The same with the videos everyone inside the Knights had been forced to watch.

Squeezing her eyes shut, she wished she could throw something. Not long before she'd fallen into a coma, the world had made sense to Ivy. Everything about dragons had been black and white. She hated and feared them. They deserved to be contained and lose their inner dragons by any nonlethal, humane way necessary.

But now? Now she had dragon doctors fighting to save her life, as well as a muscled dragonman giving her massages with strong yet gentle fingers.

And they didn't—or, according to Dr. Lewis, they couldn't—breathe fire.

The last fact shouldn't make such a difference, but Ivy had always had a thing for threes. And with three things making her doubt her former beliefs, it was enough to make her want to learn more about the dragon clan she was staying with. Maybe armed with more information, she could figure out what was true and what was a lie.

As she tried to think of how the hell she could do that, someone knocked and entered before she could ask who it was.

A tall, dark-haired woman with slightly pale skin whom Ivy had seen on TV before strode inside the room. She was some kind of reporter, although Ivy couldn't remember her name.

The woman stood next to her bed and studied her. Since Ivy was tired, she merely waited to see what the woman would do.

Finally, she spoke, her accent telling Ivy that she was from somewhere down south. "You look exhausted. And whilst normally I'd let you sleep and come back to visit you again later, Zain thought you might need another human to help you understand a few things."

Ivy didn't want another person to merely tell her things. She was done with that. What she needed was to see dragons for herself, in their daily lives.

And since the doctors and Zain were the only ones who could do that, she didn't hide her impatience. "Someone helping me understand a few things is how I eventually ended up here, in a coma, for a year. Just go away and let me sleep."

The woman raised her brows. "You must not recognize me from the telly, so let me tell you. I'm Jane Hartley, a former reporter and one of the most stubborn humans you'll ever meet. And considering my mate can be even stub-borner than I—he's in charge of security for Stonefire—

don't try to outlast me. I'll win in the end. And today? Well, today you're going to listen to me and as many other humans as it takes to start to break through the lies you believe."

Ivy muttered, "I'm already working on that and don't need your help."

Jane tilted her head a second before she sat down. "How is that possible?"

She looked away. "It's not important."

"Of course it is. Especially since your former friends drugged my teenage sister-in-law, imprisoned her along-side children half her age, and silenced her dragon for months."

At that, Ivy met Jane's gaze again. "I didn't want to hurt any children."

Jane studied her a beat before replying, "I think I believe you. But regardless, if you think dragons can breathe fire, then you have a lot to learn, Ivy Passmore. And lucky for you, I have an introductory video series about dragon-shifters. Maybe we should start there."

"No, no videos. Videos lied to me before, so why won't those ones? Until I can get out of this room and see things for myself, I don't trust anyone or anything."

Jane tsked. "And you've just lied to me, Ivy. You trusted Zain with that password and it unlocked more files than just those about the organizational structure of the Dragon Knights. One of the newly accessible files detailed the specifications of a special formula. And thanks to that, our doctors are able to create a vaccine that will protect against most of the chemicals devised before you left the Knights. Now, would you give that information to just anyone? Or, only to someone you marginally trusted?"

She ignored the small thrill at learning Zain had shared the password. "It's not about trust, but quid pro quo. I gave Zain something so he'll want to help me. That's all."

"I see." Jane stood. "Well, me, as well the other humans, will visit you fairly regularly, so prepare yourself."

Her brows knitted together. "I thought you were here to break through lies or some such thing?"

Jane shrugged. "I was, and I'll be back. But I've learned what I needed to know for today. So rest, Ivy. Someone else will probably be by again shortly."

With that, the tall woman exited the room.

Just what had the reporter been up to?

Not that she could care about it for long. Ivy struggled to keep her eyes open and, all too soon, fell back asleep.

STANDING IN A NEARBY ROOM, Zain watched Ivy's video feed.

Jane had seemed to get under the human's skin, and he wasn't sure if that was a good or bad thing.

His dragon spoke up. *Jane isn't known for tiptoeing around people. And since she's out to determine something, she'll do whatever it takes to find out what she needs.*

And yet I have to be gentle with her?

Jane is human, like Ivy. So it's less scary for Ivy than if a tall, muscled dragon-shifter interrogates her.

Zain wanted to say in that case, Jane should just take over his job, but he held back. It was unfair to burden one of the human females who had worked so hard to get other humans to like Stonefire and the other dragon-shifters of the world.

But he might need to use Jane again if Ivy didn't open up to him in the near future. He'd keep that option in his pocket for later.

Jane entered and spoke without preamble. "See? I told you. She trusts you more than you think. You've gotten quite a bit out of her in such a short time. So now you need to spend even more time in her company to find out how to decode the remaining encrypted data. The password she gave you was only the first step."

He raised his brows. "I may respect you, Jane, but you're not my boss. Be careful with your orders."

Jane rolled her eyes. "Dragon males." She met his gaze again. "You know I'm right. So instead of trying to fit me into the dominance pecking order, just find a way to get her to trust you completely. Maybe then we can understand both her and more of the Dragon Knights' methods. Although there's one more thing I want to know." Jane studied him a second before asking, "Is she your true mate?"

He blinked. "What? Where the fuck did that come from?"

The human shrugged. "Just curious. You seem fairly interested in her, and that could be the reason why."

The idea was ridiculous, but still Zain wanted to

know the truth, so he nudged his dragon until his beast woke up from dozing. Then he asked his beast, *Is she our true mate?*

His dragon yawned. *I don't know. Between the drugs and her brainwashing, the true female inside her hasn't shown herself. Until she does, I can't tell you.*

The fact there was even the slightest chance she could be his true mate made Zain's stomach churn. *She can't be. Even if she is, I don't want someone like her.*

His beast grunted. *We won't know either way for a while. But just in case she turns out to be ours, maybe don't try to make her hate us? Because even if you don't want her, I may still do. And since you won't drug me, you'll lose the battle to stay away from her in the end.*

Zain mentally grunted. *We'll see about that, dragon.*

Jane's throat clearing garnered his attention once more. Zain finally replied, "I don't know if she is or not."

The human tapped her chin. "Well, well, isn't that interesting? It'd make quite the story, you know. Former enemy turned dragon's mate. If that turns out to be the case, then you'll need to let me do a piece about you two."

He growled. "Just leave me alone, Jane. Don't you have someone else to bother?"

"Maybe." She turned toward the door but looked over her shoulder to meet his gaze again. "Just don't dismiss it before you know for sure, Zain. And even if she isn't your true mate, it's okay to like her. Some of us fight for love and tell fate to fuck off."

Kai and Jane weren't true mates but were just as devoted—maybe more so—than many true mates inside Stonefire. He muttered, "I don't bloody love anyone."

She tilted her head. "Ivy risked a lot by coming here with that thumb drive, regardless of her own personal reasons for doing so. When you think of her, start there."

The human female left, and he turned back toward the screen to stare at Ivy's sleeping form.

True, Ivy had ventured into Stonefire's territory on foot, risking her life to pass on the Dragon Knights' information.

However, he doubted it was for purely selfless reasons.

Zain suspected it was related to her brother's death.

So at the first opportunity, he'd have to open that wound and find out more.

Chapter Six

A little over a week passed, with no sign of Zain anywhere. No visits to Ivy, no messages. Nothing.

And considering she was trapped in a hospital bed, she had more than enough time to imagine every possibility as to why he hadn't returned.

Even the massages and moving of her limbs had been passed off to the nurses.

Which meant she had no idea if Zain's team had recovered all the encoded information from the password she'd provided or not, let alone if the doctors, security team, and even Stonefire's clan leader would use it as she hoped. Everyone simply told her they couldn't share anything about that yet.

If that uncertainty wasn't enough, Ivy also hadn't had the chance to convince Zain of what her ultimate end goal was. No one else had come close to listening and believing her, let alone had been willing to get her a meeting with the two IT guys working on the encrypted data. Her gut said Zain was the key to her accomplishing anything.

Ivy resisted a sigh. It wasn't as if she could go seek him out on her own. Walking was weeks away—even with the mysterious shots Dr. Sid had administered to make her heal faster—and no one was going to put her in a wheelchair and roll her right over to Zain's house, either.

Which meant waiting for him to show up again was her only option. Of course, that could take bloody weeks for all she knew.

She desperately needed a distraction.

Crossing her arms over her chest, Ivy eyed the stack of books next to her bed and debated if she was finally prepared to read them. One of them had supposedly been written by one of the human women on Stonefire —Melanie Hall-MacLeod. The other book was a first-hand account of life with dragon-shifters in Canada.

But even if Dr. Sid and Dr. Lewis both claimed the books were factual and not fabricated, Ivy had trouble trusting any nonfiction book nowadays.

Which left her with two not-so-great choices to fill her time—more TV soap operas or books that may or may not be full of lies.

What she wouldn't give for a chemistry journal. At least with science, formulas didn't lie.

Just as Ivy reached for the book set in Canada—the foreign country would at least put some distance between her and who she was reading about—the door opened.

Ivy steeled herself for someone from the medical

staff, but instead, two children raced inside and stopped at the foot of her bed.

The girl had flushed pale skin and curly blonde hair past her shoulders, which bounced as she hopped from foot to foot. The boy was calmer, with slightly lighter skin and short, dark hair.

The girl spoke first, her accent from somewhere in the North. "She doesn't look very dangerous."

The boy grunted and said with the same accent as almost everyone else on Stonefire, "She used to be a Dragon Knight. I told you what they do to dragon-shifters. They even shot Dr. Sid with a dart, which made her dragon go crazy."

The girl pointed toward her. "But she can't even get out of bed. Is that why your uncle finally said we could see her?"

Uncle? Wanting some answers, Ivy raised a hand, and both children fell silent. Ivy asked, "Who are you?"

The girl stood taller. "I'm Daisy, and that's my best friend, Freddie. We're putting on a play soon. Maybe if you get better, you can come watch. It's going to be brilliant."

Freddie frowned. "I don't want her to come. She'll ruin it."

Ivy opened her mouth, but Daisy beat her to it. "No, I don't think so. I mean, the worst she can do is shout. And maybe make noise. But she won't hurt us." The little girl looked right at Ivy. "Right? Freddie's older brother said you're trying to help Stonefire now. So I think that means you don't want to hurt dragons anymore. Which is good, because they're amazing."

Ivy blinked. Were the boy and girl dragon-shifter children? If so, who had sent them? While she understood it was probably to try and rub in how awful she'd been in trying to take away the inner dragons of nameless children, right now she lacked the energy to deal with them. "Who's the uncle? And why are you here, exactly?"

Freddie motioned toward the door. "My Uncle Zain is in the hallway. I can get him if you want. I didn't even want to come, but Daisy kept asking, and asking, and asking. So I finally said fine."

So the boy was a dragon-shifter. Or, that was the logical deduction. The ability to shift into a dragon was dominant, and dragons didn't adopt human children or suddenly become uncles to them, either.

Just as she was about to ask the boy to fetch Zain, the little girl spoke up again. "Why did you hate dragons so much? I'm human, like you. And Freddie is not only a dragon-shifter, but my bestest friend in the world. We don't have to pick one or the other. We can all be friends."

Ah, how simple the world was for a child.

Although, as Ivy tried to think of how to explain it, words failed her.

How did one explain the videos, the books, the images of destruction and death to a child?

A small voice at the back of her mind whispered, *If they're even true.*

Zain strode into the room and said, "You want to be friends with everyone, Daisy. But not all people are that accepting."

Daisy frowned. "Not with everyone. I don't like mean people."

Before she could stop herself, Ivy smiled at the girl's tone.

Zain cleared his throat, and Ivy was surprised at how his expression turned a touch exasperated. "Right, no mean people. Noted. Now, are you going to give your gift? Otherwise, it's time to leave."

Daisy's face lit up and she bobbed her head. "I forgot." She turned toward Ivy. "I forget a lot, but that's okay. I usually remember later." The little girl reached into her bag and pulled out a scrapbook and held it out to Ivy. "This is from my time at Dragon Camp. It was brilliant, with all the human and dragon kids being together." She lowered her voice. "I even saw Freddie's dragon for the first time then."

Ivy glanced at the little boy, whose cheeks were dark red.

Daisy spoke again, garnering Ivy's attention. "But I wanted to show you how much fun it is to play with dragon-shifters. So I made this scrapbook." Ivy had yet to take it, but the little girl laid it on the bed and opened it, the pictures facing toward Ivy. "See? Here we're making bracelets with our names in the old dragon language. It's a bunch of funny symbols, but no other kids in my school have them." She flipped the page. "And here, they let us slide down the side of an adult dragon! That was the best. Well, tied for the best. Seeing Freddie's dragon was brilliant, too."

As the little girl kept talking, explaining one page

after the other, Ivy wondered if all of this was a ruse to make her trust the dragons.

Or, could it be the truth?

Because if it was the truth, and dragon and human children were staying and playing together, all under the supervision of the DDA and with permission from human parents, Ivy's world view would shift a little. After all, according to everything within the Dragon Knights, dragons never befriended humans unless they could get something in return.

And unless the dragon-shifters were grooming children to eventually become dragon mates—which even to Ivy seemed a bit farfetched—they were welcoming humans on their land with little to gain. Sure, maybe there would be some positive PR, but as she watched the little boy move closer to the little girl and help her explain the pictures, Ivy sensed a true friendship between them.

Ivy needed some answers of her own. Maybe the children were extremely talented actors, but given how Daisy flitted from one topic to another and didn't always finish her thought, Ivy doubted it.

Which meant she needed to take advantage of the children—they could be brutally honest, and she needed that. So at the next pause she could pounce on, Ivy asked, "Daisy, whilst I know you like dragon-shifters, does everyone you know accept them, too?"

Daisy sighed. "No. I lost my old best friend, Lucy. Her mum doesn't like dragons and wouldn't let me play with her anymore."

Ivy pushed on. "If you could go back to Lucy

tomorrow and be best friends again, would you stop seeing the dragon-shifters?"

Ivy could feel Zain's gaze on her, but she ignored it and waited for Daisy's answer.

ZAIN WAITED to see how his nephew's friend would answer.

He didn't have to let Daisy reply, of course. He could tell Daisy and Freddie to go back to the surgery's lobby, where Nikki—another Protector—waited for them. However, he was curious. The question wouldn't harm the child, and Daisy had a way of winning people over without even trying or realizing it. If she could win over Ivy, it could go a long way toward the human female working with Stonefire to eradicate the Dragon Knights.

His dragon spoke up. *It might also help Ivy like us instead of hate us.*

That doesn't matter to me, only you.

His beast huffed and fell silent as Daisy finally shook her head and answered Ivy's question. "No, I wouldn't go back and do that. I miss Lucy every day, and probably always will. But I've made so many friends here playing with the dragons, both human and dragon. Not to mention Freddie and me have plans to help Stonefire. And to do that, we need lots of time together. Right, Freddie?"

Freddie merely shrugged, which was enough for Daisy because she added, "And besides, my mum says that sometimes we have to make choices about things. It's not always easy, and we might be sad sometimes, but if we pick the one that makes us happy for the future, then we'll be less sad later. I think that's what will happen eventually with me. Picking Freddie and the others here will make me happy for a long time."

Daisy and Freddie shared a look—the pair liked to conspire, which probably didn't bode well for whomever was the target—but Zain let them be. His sister and Daisy's mum could worry about the pair's troublemaking.

Instead, Zain watched Ivy.

The little crease between her brows spoke volumes. He suspected she was starting to doubt more and more what she'd learned inside the Dragon Knights.

Although he needed to do a little poking of his own, to see how far that doubt had settled. So he looked at his nephew. "Freddie, I think it's time for you to take Daisy home for lunch." Daisy opened her mouth to protest—the little girl never cared about dominance or hierarchies and would become a headache when she was older—but Zain beat her to it. "No, Daisy. You promised to leave when it was time. If you break your promise, then Freddie's mum won't let you wander around Stonefire with Alfie and Freddie for the rest of your current visit."

Alfie was Zain's other nephew, who was old enough to watch the pair and keep them out of the worst trouble.

Daisy dropped her head with an exaggerated sigh. But she quickly bounced back and pushed the scrapbook toward Ivy. "Look at all the pictures, and maybe I can come back and tell you some more stories." She lowered her voice dramatically. "We even had special drills during the camp, where we had to wait underground until any danger was gone."

Not wanting the little girl to reveal Stonefire's emergency procedures, Zain moved to the side of the two kids and gently turned them toward the door. "That's enough. Go to Nikki so she can take you home for some lunch."

The pair waved, and then Freddie managed to get Daisy to leave.

How his nephew controlled that bundle of nonstop energy, Zain had no idea.

As soon as the door closed, Ivy's voice filled the room. "Why did you bring them here?"

He turned toward the human, who was holding the scrapbook against her chest. While she was still pale and too thin, it was good to see she'd regained some strength. Otherwise, his volunteering to give her some of his blood would've been pointless.

His dragon hummed but didn't say anything. Zain already knew his beast liked that the female had their blood in her veins.

He tried not to think of why.

Ignoring his dragon, Zain answered Ivy, "I could say I brought them because Daisy kept asking to see you."

"You could, but that's not it entirely. What's the full truth?"

"The full truth?" He took a step closer to the bed. "I thought maybe you'd believe her over me. Daisy loves dragon-shifters almost more than any other human I've ever met. And even though it's cost her and her mother quite a bit back in their city—both with friends and neighbors—Daisy keeps coming back with her mother's blessing. I figure if a little girl could sacrifice so much and still want to see us, you might believe her over books and videos."

Ivy silently stared down at the scrapbook for a few beats before speaking again. "I-I don't know what to think anymore."

Maybe some of the other Protectors would step back when seeing the human so unsure and fragile.

But not Zain. He'd given her a week to regain enough strength to face his questions. Mostly because of Trahern's orders, but also because Zain hadn't wanted to fight the Welsh dragon doctor on the issue.

And after waiting—always the bloody waiting—it was finally time to find out the answers he needed. "Then tell me why you came to Stonefire. Was it only because the Knights killed your brother, Richard, and you wanted revenge? Or, is there more to it?"

One second ticked by, and then another. Even knowing that Serafina was watching them via the video feed didn't make Zain rush the human. With the doctors attending a meeting with Stonefire's clan leader, there was no one to barge in and tell him to leave. And Zain wasn't going anywhere until she answered him.

AT THE MENTION of Richard's death, Ivy kept her gaze trained on the scrapbook in her arms and willed for her tears not to fall.

She'd done her best to face her grief, but hearing

Richard's name had tumbled most of the walls she'd built around her pain.

Playing with the side of the scrapbook, running her nail back and forth, Ivy took a deep breath and slowly pushed away the grief. It would come back later, but she only needed to keep it away long enough to get Zain to leave her alone.

When she was fairly sure she could meet his gaze without breaking down, Ivy lifted her head and looked the dragonman in the eyes. Eyes that were neutral, free of any emotion. After another few seconds, she asked, "Why are you asking me that?"

He shrugged one shoulder. "Because it's my job to do so."

She stared at the dragon-shifter. Ivy should be angry at him for poking her still grieving heart. And yet, his straightforwardness was refreshing. Unlike the medical staff, he didn't try to ignore her or ask the bare minimum. No, Zain wanted to know more about her.

Sure, it was for his own ends and would probably determine her eventual fate, but after abandoning the life she'd known for years and losing her brother and his partner on top of it, Ivy desperately needed someone to treat her as more than some hated enemy.

Besides, it wasn't as if she had anything to lose by telling him about Richard's murder. If anything, he might be more open to the request she needed to make.

Putting aside the scrapbook, she answered, "My brother and his partner were killed by the Dragon Knights. And whilst I have no hard evidence beyond a symbol drawn on the wall, I know they did it because my brother took me in after I ran away from the Knights."

"So he was murdered, then."

Ivy tried not to read too much into how Zain's voice was a little softer than before. "Yes." Not wanting to cry again, she looked down toward the blanket and picked at it. "I'm the one that found them. But I couldn't tell the police everything, even though I burned to."

"Why?"

There was zero reason to reveal how the police had moles inside their organization, ones that would pass on any information to the Knights.

And yet, what good was keeping the information to herself now? So she explained it and added, "That's why I reported it but didn't reveal how it was my fault they'd been killed. The thumb drive full of information had been my insurance against the Knights coming after me. But in the end, it wasn't enough to protect the ones I loved."

Tears prickled her eyes and she took a few deep breaths to hold them back. She wouldn't—couldn't—cry in front of this dragonman.

After a few seconds, Zain's voice filled the room again. "Is there information on the thumb drive about the spies inside the police?"

She blinked and met his gaze again. "You believe me?"

He grunted noncommittally. "Maybe. However, if there's detailed information we can use, then tell me how to access it."

Here it was—her chance to ask for a meeting with

the IT people. "I could, or you could bring the men or women working on decrypting the data, and I could tell them how to do it."

Zain shook his head, and her hope vanished. He replied, "No, not yet. Whilst Daisy may be overly forgiving and see the good in you without batting an eyelash, it's not the same with the adults. It's better if you go through me for now."

She suspected he wanted to be the only main contact she had within the dragon clan. While she wasn't trying to deceive anyone, no doubt the dragons were still on alert regarding anything to do with her.

However, Ivy wanted more than just talking with an interrogator. She yearned for some kind of contact, to remind her that she was alive and might, just might, find a way to avenge her brother and do some good instead of harm in the world.

Yes, Richard deserved justice. It was the very least she could do considering his patience and accepting her back without a word. It was partly because of his suggestion to ask the dragon-shifters for help that she'd gathered the courage to venture north to Stonefire.

Using her brother's memory for courage, Ivy blurted, "Then let the children visit me again. Agree to that, and I'll dictate the step-by-step instructions on how to access the police-related files."

Zain raised his brows. "That's not what I thought you'd ask for. But all the same, it's up to their parents. If they agree, I'll bring them. If not, I won't force them."

She bobbed her head. "I'll take what I can get."

Zain took out his mobile phone, tapped it a few

times, and moved closer to her bed. While she knew he was standing, which of course, made him taller, she had to strain her neck to look at his face.

And as he leaned over, his heat and scent washed over her. She should be bothered about his nearness, but his closeness just felt…right. As if he should be by her side as often as possible.

What? He's a dragon. That's crazy. The comfort vanished, replaced with the desire to race to the other side of the room. Just because a few kids had made her at least question some of her beliefs surrounding dragon-shifters, she wasn't about to jump into bed with one.

Not that she would be sleeping with anyone for quite a while, if ever. But a dragon-shifter would be at the bottom of that list.

Zain grunted. "I'm going to record you. Are you ready?"

She finally met his gaze again and did her best not to gasp at his flashing pupils.

The slits gave him a reptilian appearance, and at one time the sight would've stirred a mixture of fear and hatred.

But now, she watched the change with curiosity. Inner dragons were supposed to speak to their human halves. However, she had no idea what they talked about. The Knights have always said it was instructions for the human halves to find women to impregnate or to kill any human who challenged them.

Given how the dragonman stood next to her bed, holding his phone out and waiting to record her voice, she had a hard time believing that was the truth.

Without thinking, she asked, "What is your dragon saying?"

He frowned, and his pupils turned round and remained that way. "Nothing of importance. I don't know how long I have before the medical staff return, so tell our team how to access the files."

So much for finding out more concerning inner dragons. Maybe the kids would tell her more, if they ever came to visit again.

And while she was ready to give Zain the instructions, there was one more thing they all needed to be careful of. "Just don't share this information with the DDA, okay? They aren't as trustworthy as you think they are."

His eyes flashed again before he grunted. "Fine. Just hurry up and tell me what I need to know."

Her instinct was to dig in her heels and say nothing. However, Ivy forced herself to give the instructions on how to decrypt and read the police-related files.

Once she finished, Zain tapped his phone a few times and left without another word.

All she could do now was wait and hope Zain shared the information right away. Both she and the dragon-shifters would benefit if he did so.

Not that she could order the man to do anything. So she leaned back against her pillows and exhaustion set in, making it hard to sit upright.

However, Ivy hated going to sleep and tried to fight the heaviness of her eyelids. Even now, after how many days of waking up without a problem, she worried about falling into a coma again. One she might not shake off the next time.

And given everything the doctors had shared with her about being poisoned by the Knights and how fragile her health was, she didn't take being awake lightly.

Fighting the heaviness of her limbs, she managed to reach for the scrapbook and opened it. There was a picture of Freddie, Daisy, and another little girl holding up their paintings. While none of them were very talented, Ivy could tell they were paintings of dragons.

But the art wasn't what caught her eye. No, she focused on their smiles. They were so happy.

Would she ever achieve that sort of easy happiness again? To have fun and not worry about the next deadline or risk being put into isolation until she met it.

With a little bit of distance, Ivy wondered why she'd ever fallen in line within the Knights. There'd been no happiness, no celebrations, nothing but deadlines and fear.

Sure, a small sense of purpose and belonging, but that didn't outweigh the bad.

Stop thinking about the past, Ivy. She couldn't change it, but maybe her future would be better.

She touched the picture of the three kids. While it wasn't a guarantee, if the kids visited again, then it'd be nice to spend some time with people who didn't hate her entire existence for once. And maybe, she could finally smile for a little while, too.

Chapter Seven

Zain laid down the printed documents on the table and curled his fingers into a fist. To his boss, Kai, he muttered, "The fucking Knights have infiltrated the Cumbria police, too."

Cumbria was the county where the Lake District, which included Stonefire, was located in England. Although they were far from the only constabulary with dragon-hating sympathies. The list was longer than Zain liked, by quite a bit.

One of the other Protectors in the room—Nikki Gray, who was Kai's second-in-command—huffed. "I suspected one or two of them didn't like us. At least, in my experience, they were dismissive and condescending, as if talking with me was a waste of time. But I didn't think they'd be full-on working with a group out to eradicate us. It feels wrong keeping this knowledge in-house."

Zain stated, "But we can't tell the DDA, at least not until we know for sure if Ivy's warning is true or not."

Nikki tapped her chin. "Maybe we can't tell someone at random, but I'm sure Evie knows a few people we can trust. And Bram could probably reach out to the DDA Director. I can't imagine Rosalind Abbott being in league with the Knights, not given how hard she's been fighting for our rights and acceptance."

Kai finally raised a hand to stop their conversation and spoke. "Right now, we're not reaching out to anybody." He met Zain's gaze. "Whilst we verify some of the contents of the files, I want you to spend more time with the human. It's entirely possible she's the best actor in the world and is feeding us the information we want to hear."

It was a possibility, certainly, although both Zain's gut and dragon said she wasn't that nefarious. Still, he asked, "What about her brother's murder? Do you think she would be part of that, too?"

Kai raised his blond eyebrows. "It wouldn't surprise me if some of the Knights would sacrifice their family members for a greater cause."

Zain tried to imagine Ivy suggesting they murder her brother so that the dragon-shifters would believe her.

But then he remembered the tears in her eyes, the defeated slump of her shoulders, and the hovering regret that flashed in her eyes when she thought no one was looking. He never would've believed he'd defend the human, but Zain said, "I don't think she suggested or agreed with that plan. I've been watching her on the video feed for nearly two weeks, and when she's alone, she always looks sad. Considering she has no idea we have a camera inside her room, you would think that she'd lower her guard when she's alone."

Leaning back in his chair, Kai's pupils flashed before he replied, "Watching from a video feed might not be enough. Especially since there have been plenty of human spies who've lived a life of lies for decades, never letting down their facades. It's entirely possible she's doing that, too, with a highly developed persona." Kai paused a second before adding, "However, there's a better way to determine if she's telling the truth or merely acting."

Zain didn't like the glint in Kai's eyes. "I know you have a plan, so just tell us what it is already."

Kai tapped his fingers on the table. "Take her as your mate, live with her, and figure out the truth."

Zain's mouth dropped open as he tried to process Kai's words. Dragon-shifters took matings seriously, and divorce was difficult. Not to mention if he aligned himself with Ivy, a good portion of the clan would probably turn their backs on him.

It was a hell of a lot to ask of him for an assignment that might not give them the answers or proof they needed.

When he finally made his mouth work again, Zain growled, "I know you and Jane have made comments about me finding a mate of my own, but this is fucking ridiculous."

Nikki leaned forward and said, "It's a brilliant idea, though. You could find out all she knows, watch her closely to see if she's being genuine or not, and not even Dr. Sid could limit your time at her side like she can now.

Unless your reputation and popularity are more important to you than discovering the key to take down one of our enemies?"

Zain narrowed his eyes at Nikki. The female could lay it on thick when she tried. "Would you mate a former Dragon Knight or dragon hunter just to get information?"

She waved a hand in dismissal. "That's a moot point, isn't it? I'm already mated and have a daughter to boot. I'm most definitely off the market."

He was tempted to challenge Nikki to a set of grueling flight routines so he could kick her arse in the only way her human mate would allow.

Kai rapped the table with his knuckles. "This isn't about Nikki. I could ask one of the other Protectors, but you're the most skilled at reading body language, not to mention my top interrogator. And the human is getting more comfortable around you, too. Face it—this is the best option, and you know it. Besides, it's not like you'd have to fuck her, just live with her."

His dragon perked up. *Why wouldn't we fuck her? That's the best part of mating—to always have a sex partner.*

Whilst you may be on board to sleep with anything that has a vagina, I have some standards. Murderous zealots are most definitely not part of them.

Kai's voice prevented Zain's dragon from replying. "Just think about it. I'll ask you again tomorrow and make plans from there."

Would a day really change his reaction and heart? Not really.

However, while he'd like to deny it with all he had,

the plan *was* his best chance at finding out everything concerning Ivy Passmore.

And the sooner he did that, the sooner his clan could plan to dismantle and destroy the Dragon Knights once and for all.

In other words, to complete his mission, he'd have to sacrifice his own wishes for a little while. And it wasn't as if it was permanent. He could eventually obtain a divorce.

As for being shunned, once he could reveal his role and the reason for doing it—to take down and end the fear surrounding one of their enemies—the clan members who ostracized him would welcome him back again.

His dragon grunted. *If they don't stand by us during the tough times, then why bother with them later?*

So I tell Kai no then? Being shunned isn't the easiest thing to endure when you're supposed to protect the entire clan.

We can still do our job. And it's not as if you are Mister Social Butterfly to begin with.

Zain mentally sighed. *You're going to keep going until I agree to this, aren't you?*

Of course. Besides, think of it this way—having Ivy around is one step closer to sleeping with a female than where we are now.

And people thought human males thought about sex all the time. Inner dragons were so much worse.

Before his beast could say a word—let alone before Zain lost his resolve—he blurted, "I'll do it. Although I have a few conditions."

Kai bobbed his head. "Then let's hear them."

As Zain ran through what he wanted, he tried to

ignore the small ball of anticipation buzzing around his stomach.

Not because he was looking forward to mating the female. No, that was bloody ridiculous. It was for the ultimate goal of taking down a long-time enemy, and nothing more.

IVY HAD JUST FINISHED her lunch—what she wouldn't give to have a pizza or curry again instead of the soft, bland cuisine they fed her—when someone knocked on the door. Fully expecting Dr. Sid or Dr. Innes, she said, "Come in."

The door opened, revealing a tall woman with olive skin, brown eyes, and black hair down to her waist. A slightly different but familiar style of tattoo peeked out from her short-sleeved top. Before she could stop herself, Ivy asked, "Are you a dragon-shifter?"

The woman smiled, nodded, and shut the door behind her. "Yes, I am. My name is Dr. Serafina Rossi."

Her English was perfect but slightly accented. Combined with her name and looks, Ivy guessed she was from Italy. "Another doctor? Well, what are you here for then? I don't think there's much more blood left in me to draw."

"No, I'm not that kind of doctor." She took a step closer to Ivy's bed. "I'm a psychologist."

Ivy had never really thought much about shrinks before she'd been lured in by the Friends of the World. But given those therapists had brainwashed her into joining the Dragon Knights, Ivy assessed the woman warily. "I don't need your help."

Serafina tilted her head. "I expected you to say that."

She studied the other woman. "Then why are you here?"

The dragonwoman shrugged. "I've been working with Zain on your case and felt it was time for me to talk with you."

She'd suspected people talked about her behind her back, but it appeared people were doing more than merely gossiping. Ivy asked, "Why now? I've been awake for nearly two weeks."

Serafina raised her dark brows. "Would you have listened to me during the first few days?"

"No," she mumbled.

"Right, so I waited, watched, and listened. You've come far in such a short time, but your life will have many more changes soon, so I thought we should chat."

She searched the dragonwoman's gaze. "What changes?"

Serafina waved around the room. "You won't be in this hospital bed forever, right? Once you can walk again, what will you do? Where will you go? Unless the Knights are defeated, the second you step off of Stonefire, they'll find you and eradicate one of their weaknesses."

Ivy had never thought of herself as one of the Knights' weaknesses, but given the data she'd stolen, she probably was a bigger threat than she'd realized. Back when she'd stolen it, the data had only been a means of securing safety.

Which had failed.

Richard. Images of her older brother laughing, his partner teasing Ivy, and the three of them enjoying some time on the Brighton Pier in the summer came rushing back.

Serafina's soft voice broke through her memories. "You're thinking of your brother, aren't you?"

Her gaze shot to the dragonwoman's. "Why would you say that?"

"Given everything I've read, he and his partner were your only family, your only weaknesses. Well, unless you're secretly pining to return to the Knights."

"Never," she growled, the intensity surprising even herself.

Serafina bobbed her head. "I thought so, and your response is believable. However, you're going to have to work hard to convince everyone of how that is the truth."

Ivy should say nothing and merely tell the dragonwoman what she wanted to hear. That would get her out of her room as quickly as possible.

And yet anger flooded her body. Anger at what she'd done to her brother, at the Knights for using and disposing of her, and even anger at no one believing her when she was being bloody sincere.

She'd done awful things, and would always have to live with that. But Ivy was trying her best to make up for it, and no one seemed to notice or give a shit.

And while Serafina hadn't said anything that others hadn't said already, something snapped inside Ivy. "What else do I bloody need to do? I nearly died coming here with information you lot needed. Then I lost a year of my life to a coma, courtesy of some unknown drug the

Knights gave me. And then I've been offering information whenever asked of me. Do I need to cut off one of
my legs to prove how serious I am? Or, do I need to
charge into battle and help take down the Knights myself
before anyone gives me a chance? Tell me, Dr. Rossi,
what's the magical next step I need to take on my road of
recovery?"

The dragonwoman didn't miss a beat. "With the clan,
that's easy—give them all the information needed to
decrypt the data you brought."

"I already offered to do that, but Zain said I couldn't
meet with the men or women in charge of that task."

Serafina folded her arms across her chest. "Then I'll
see what I can arrange. But the other aspect, to come to
terms with what you've done internally, within yourself,
will be much harder."

Ivy didn't think she'd ever be able to forgive herself
for what had happened to her brother and David.
Nothing would bring either of them back from the dead.

However, she was in such a mood that she motioned
with her hand and demanded, "Then tell me your
advice, Doctor."

"You'll need to grieve properly, first and foremost.
And commit to regular sessions with me. I think you need
at least one person you can be yourself with and not hide
anything. And since you're my patient, I won't hold judgment. Every step I take will be based on what I think
needs to be done to help you heal."

Ivy growled, "Which is close to what the Friends of
the World told me, back when they first lured me in to try
and get me into the Dragon Knights."

Serafina tilted her head. "And whilst the Protectors will want to hear more of that process with the Friends of the World, I'm more concerned about you. I'm a fully licensed psychologist, unlike those fake ones you dealt with before. My goal isn't to brainwash. No, it's quite the opposite—to help you see the world through your own eyes."

For a split second, Ivy yearned to have someone she could unload to, a person to talk with who wouldn't growl, condescend, or outright speak with hatred toward her.

And yet, the thought of baring so much of herself to Serafina made her nervous. The Knights had used the information from her sessions against her over the years, to keep her in line. Not only that, but her personal revelations had probably also led them straight to her brother and his partner.

However, this time, Ivy had nothing to lose. No family, no friends. Not even a few quid to her name.

With nothing to lose, she shrugged and said, "Fine. But not today. I need time to wrap my head around talking with anyone about some of the worst parts of myself."

Serafina stood and bobbed her head. "I wasn't planning on talking with you today, anyway. But request me at any time, Ivy. I have a feeling you'll need me sooner than you think."

With that cryptic statement, Serafina exited the room, leaving Ivy alone again before she could ask about meeting with the IT personnel working on her thumb drive data.

She'd have to make that request again as soon as possible.

However, as Ivy sat in her bed and stared at the blank wall, it was hard to believe she'd really just agreed to talk with Serafina on a regular basis, most likely baring her soul in the process.

The only positive was that it was true—Ivy didn't have anything to lose. No, she only had things to gain. Namely, the ability to grieve and vent on occasion. It'd take some time to get to the harder stuff, such as her massive guilt and maybe even overcoming it one day.

And it wasn't as if she had any friends with the dragons she could do that with.

So if no one wanted to talk to her simply because she tried to be better and reach out, then she'd take whatever she could get. Even Ivy could get lonely, and the nurses and sparse visits from Zain and a few others weren't nearly enough.

Only time would tell if her sessions with Serafina made any fucking difference to her situation on Stonefire.

Chapter Eight

The next morning Ivy had barely finished her physical therapy session with Nurse Ginny when Zain waltzed into the room.

She'd planned on asking about the kids visiting her again, but something about the determination in his unwavering gaze made her voice die in her throat.

He stopped next to her bed and continued to stare, as if he'd never seen her before.

True, the nurses had used some special dry shampoo to take away the greasiness of her hair, but it wasn't as if her slightly cleaner appearance would attract the dragon-man's notice.

He nodded and then said, "Today's your lucky day, Ivy Passmore."

Something about his eyes flashing made her wary. She asked cautiously, "Why?"

"Because you're gaining a mate, which means you'll

be safe from the DDA for a while, as well as the other clan members."

A mate was the term dragons used for their spouses, and she nearly snorted at the absurdity of Zain's statement. "Stop joking around and wasting time, Zain. I'd rather discuss if you accessed the information on the corrupt police officers or not?"

He grunted. "We did, and we'll talk more about that later. But I'm not joking, Ivy. We're to be mated later today."

She blinked. "What?"

"No, I'm not about to profess some sort of secret love for you. But now that you're awake, it's only a matter of time before someone leaks to the DDA that you're here. So we're being proactive."

Too many thoughts whirred through her brain, and all she could manage to say was "I can't marry a dragon-shifter."

Zain leaned forward, his eyes mere inches away. "You can, and you will."

Something about the certainty in his tone, as if he were a parent telling a child what to do, snapped her out of her shock. "I know I shouldn't look a gift horse in the mouth, but even if I were to marry some dragon for protection, I would hope it was someone who doesn't obviously hate me."

He leaned even closer, to the point she could feel the heat of his breath on her face. "Hate is a strong word. Besides, this way I can keep an eye on you."

She had a feeling that was the true reason for the absurd mating suggestion.

And as Zain continued to invade her personal space, with Ivy not being able to move away, she tried to not look at his lips. She really shouldn't. However, her curiosity won out, and she instantly noticed how firm and lickable they were, as if kissing them was something she should do every day.

Not to mention the heat and scent that was uniquely Zain filled her nose, and for a few beats, her sadness, her past, all of it didn't matter. She felt…safe.

No. She had to stop falling for the dragon's strange pheromones, or whatever it was that addled her brain whenever Zain was nearby.

Ivy forced her gaze to just over his shoulder, focusing on a faded picture of a lake with mountains behind it, helping her to focus on what Zain had said and not his inarguably fit body.

If she mated him, she'd no doubt have to be near him all the time. His quiet presence studying her as if she were some sort of unique insect. Never saying something to cheer her up, or even caring about what went on through her brain.

True, she had Serafina to confide in, to a degree. But Ivy had always seen marriage—er, matings—as a serious step in her life. She may need to do it for protection, but there had to be a less intense dragon-shifter who'd do it.

She finally murmured, "There has to be someone else."

He moved away. "No, there's just me. Bram and a few witnesses will be here in a little while. And before you protest about being mated in your hospital gown, Nikki and Jane will be stopping by to help you put on something else. I have no idea what—and frankly, don't care—but you can thank Nikki for that little bit of kindness."

She forced her gaze back to his again, to the brusque man she was supposed to marry. "I don't care about looking pretty, or some sort of kindness. I'm barely getting used to you stopping by once a day. Having you around all the time will hurt my health."

He snorted. "Sure, say that. But don't worry. You've met Serafina, and she'll help you with overcoming your fear of dragons. Between her and the children visiting, your apprehensions should slowly melt away."

He spoke as if she were afraid on purpose, just to irritate him. Ivy leaned forward a little. "You can't just snap your fingers and make everything okay."

"No, but it's not as if you have a choice in the matter, do you?"

As they stared at one another, neither of them speaking, Ivy's heart rate kicked up.

The hard planes of his face should terrify her. And yet, the deep brown of his eyes drew her in, making her want to know more about him.

No. She moved as far away from him as she could manage, which wasn't much. Spending a prolonged amount of time near Zain was a bad idea, a really bad idea.

Because she could deny it, but she might start to want the dragonman if he were around all the time and showed the slightest hint of kindness.

And Ivy didn't want the temptation to distract her from her end goal of eradicating the Dragon Knights.

He slowly stood upright again. "And here's one last

thing I'll leave you with—open up to me and work with us, and I'll ensure that whoever killed your brother and his partner will be at the top of my list of Knights to find."

So now he was dangling a treat in front of her? He didn't have to, which piqued her curiosity. "Why would you promise that?"

"I want all the Knights taken down, so finding one or a small group of them isn't that much extra work."

If Ivy cooperated with the Stonefire dragons, they'd find her brother's killers eventually anyway.

However, she may never know who they were.

No, this might be the only way she could learn the names of the murderers and get some closure. Because even if she didn't know them personally, names alone would allow her to blame a specific someone or someones.

Well, mostly. Ivy would never fully be absolved of her part in it all.

Not wanting to think more about that right now, when her future was being decided, she looked at Zain. She sensed he was right—she didn't have a choice. However, Ivy had one last question before agreeing to the ridiculous plan. "It will be a legal marriage only, right?"

Zain's pupils flashed a few times before he cleared his throat and said, "Yes. Despite what the Knights may have taught you, I don't rape females for sport. If a female is in my bed, she's there willingly."

He was cocky, for sure. That was one of the few things the Knights had told her that had turned out to be true regarding dragon-shifters, at least in Zain's case. "That's a non-answer."

He raised his brows. "Only if it means you intend to show the slightest interest in being in my bed."

Ivy pulled the covers up to her shoulders even though the thin material could do nothing to protect her from the tall, muscled dragonman not more than a foot away. She cleared her throat. "That won't be a problem for me."

"Good. Then Nikki and Jane will be by shortly. The next time you see me, it'll be to mate you."

Zain exited the room, and Ivy dropped the covers as she let out a huge sigh.

If someone had told her even a few days ago that she'd be mating a dragonman, she would've laughed in their face.

True, it wasn't like she really had a choice in the matter if she wanted continued protection. However, her former colleagues would've tried to kidnap her and chain her inside a cave rather than let her go through with it.

Of course, they weren't her colleagues any longer. No, they were her enemies.

So Ivy would go through with it. But if Zain thought she'd ever share his bed, he'd be waiting a long time. Even putting aside her fears and doubts about his species, human women who birthed half-dragon-shifter babies not only had a fifty-fifty chance of dying in childbirth, they were often ostracized by a large portion of human society.

Ivy didn't want any of that. She'd spent nearly five

years of her life working in secret with the Knights, abandoning everyone she knew outside of their organization. She didn't want to have to face that all again.

Once the Knights were taken care of, then Ivy would find a way to escape and start over somewhere in the world with a new identity.

And that would be her motivation for surviving the mating ceremony and probably living with a grumpy dragonman for who knew how long.

LESS THAN AN HOUR LATER, shortly after Ivy had finally dozed off, there was a resounding knock on her door. She'd barely opened her eyes before two women entered the room.

Well, one was a human woman—Jane. The other with black hair and light golden skin had the tell-tale tattoo on her bicep of a dragon-shifter.

The dragonwoman was a little shorter than Jane, which was rare since dragon-shifters were usually really tall. Maybe her mother had been human.

Not that she would ever ask that question and risk upsetting a dragon-shifter she'd never met before.

As Ivy tried to think of what to do or say, the dragonwoman spoke up, her accent the same Northern English as everyone else originally from Stonefire. "You don't have to look at me like I'm going to eviscerate you. Maybe before I had my daughter, I'd have been tempted, but now I need to set an example. Tolerance at first meeting, and all that. But only because you gave us so much useful information." The dragonwoman stepped closer toward Ivy's bed. "Do anything to hurt my mate or daughter, though, and tolerance is out the window."

Ivy had always been taught that female dragon-shifters were weak and did whatever the men wanted. However, first with Dr. Sid and now this dragonwoman, Ivy started to believe it was another lie she needed to throw away.

Jane snorted. "Be a little nicer, Nikki. She's about to mate Zain, which means she'll get more than her fill of threats and alpha attitude."

"Hey, that's her choice, not mine." Nikki looked back at Ivy. "Besides, I was the one who lobbied for Ivy to have a real dress for her mating ceremony. I don't know about you, but I wouldn't want my arse hanging out for the occasion."

Since the pair seemed to be talking more to each other than to Ivy, she decided to jump in. "I don't care either way. It's not a real marriage."

"Mating," Jane corrected. "Regardless, I don't want to see your arse for the ceremony. And seeing as I'll be here, along with my mate, let's get you changed for my own selfish reasons."

Jane acted nonchalantly, but Ivy sensed the woman was pretending it meant nothing and wanted her to have a little normalcy for the event.

Ivy hadn't lied—she didn't care what she wore one way or the other. But as she imagined strangers staring at her backside, she did her best to sit up, albeit slowly. "Fine. Then let's hurry and get this over with."

Jane sat on the side of the bed. "Not quite yet. First,

we're going to have a chat."

Bloody great. Everyone seemed to have a talk or chat in mind. Even the children had come prepared before.

Since remaining silent and nodding was the fastest way to get it over with, Ivy did so.

Nikki laughed. "It's almost as if she knows you already, Jane. Not even fighting the dictate."

Jane raised an eyebrow. "And a word of advice, Ivy— don't do the nod and smile routine with your dragonman. Zain is stubborn and determined, and quite a private person compared to most other dragon-shifters I know. If you don't attempt to roll over him on occasion—speaking your mind and not backing down—you'll never learn anything about him."

She frowned. "Why would I even want to? As soon as everyone gets what they need from me, he'll divorce me. I think dragon-shifters divorce, don't they?"

Nikki bobbed her head. "They do, but it's rare. However, if you end up being Zain's true mate, something he won't know until you're not pumped full of drugs and you're finally healthy again, he might not grant you one."

Ivy blinked. "Wait, what are you talking about? A dragon sees their true mate, claims them whether they're willing or not, and then takes the child and tosses the woman aside until he's ready for another offspring. I can't be Zain's since he hasn't done any of those things."

Nikki raised her brows. "Is that the rubbish they teach you? No wonder you lot hate us so much. My true mate is human, by the way. And if you ask Rafe, he'll confirm that I didn't rape him to conceive a child." She smiled secretly. "The conceiving a child bit can be the fun part, if done right."

She blinked. "Your mate is human? I didn't think human men could be with a dragonwoman."

Jane shared a glance with Nikki before the woman said to Ivy, "They did a real number on you, didn't they? I have half a mind to tell Zain to wait to mate you until Nikki, me, and probably Mel and Evie sit you down and tell you the truth about living with a dragon-shifter."

Ivy recognized one of the names. "Melanie Hall-MacLeod. She wrote that book, the fictional one to make dragons look good."

Jane frowned. "No, it's all true. I heard about the books they forced you to read, and after reading excerpts myself from the files you brought us, I can start to see why you fear dragons so much. But it's all rubbish, Ivy. Mel loves Tristan, and whilst Tristan can be a grumpy arsehole to the rest of us, he adores Melanie and his children. You should see it for yourself."

Ivy looked from Jane to Nikki and back again. Were they telling the truth? Had everything she'd ever learned about dragon-shifters from the Knights been a lie?

Closing her eyes, she placed a hand on her forehead and took a few deep breaths. Most of the people she'd met on Stonefire seemed so normal. And the majority of them were happy, and even liked to joke around.

Surely an entire clan couldn't be playacting and merely trying to deceive her.

Maybe the dragon-shifters and their mates were just like humans elsewhere in the world. They loved, lived, and tried their best to make it through the day.

But if that was the truth, then Ivy had hurt so many people under false beliefs, some of those people hurt irrevocably. After all, she'd been the head drug researcher for years before leaving the Knights. It was only because of her formulas that the dragons had finally started to weaken.

And considering she'd been unconscious for a year, then who knew what the Knights had come up with during that time.

The dragon-shifters could be in real danger.

Ivy could help them with more than decrypting the files; she could share antidotes, or at the very least, have a leg up at developing them to any new strains that had appeared while she'd been in a coma. But could she bring herself to help the dragons? Could she make the jump and believe the dragon-shifters weren't out to rape and kill humans on a whim, with their sole goal to take over the world?

She rubbed her forehead again, even though it did nothing to ease the pain inside her brain and heart.

Nikki's soft voice reached her ears. "I know all of this is too much too soon. And if I'm being honest, we were supposed to hold back more than we have. But I say rubbish to that. Friends of mine have suffered because of the Knights. If there's even a small chance that me telling you a few things will help to sway your mind, then I'm going to do it and keep doing it. Because as much as we may have hated each other in the past, we can do a lot of good in the future if we work together. You might even be able to redeem yourself to the clan and have somewhere to belong."

Ivy lowered her hand, opened her eyes, and met Nikki's dark brown gaze. She barely even noticed the flashing pupils, a true testament to how far she'd come in such a short time. And for the first time, Ivy saw Nikki as just another person instead of a potential enemy out to harm as many humans as possible.

And even if the dragons did toss her out eventually, Ivy had a lot to make up for. She couldn't bring her brother or his partner back, let alone repair all the damage she'd done with her chemical compounds. However, she could arm the dragon-shifters with as much knowledge as possible to take down the Knights, who were the real villains.

Nikki put out a hand as if to shake. "Will you help us, Ivy? I know you're not strong enough yet, but if you promise now to help us, then Jane and I will work on getting you some time away from Zain and exposing you to others inside the clan."

Ivy stared at Nikki's hand. It should be simple to lift her arm and shake—she'd regained enough strength to do it—but she hesitated.

She'd been awake for about two weeks, and her mind whirred with all sorts of contradictions regarding the dragon-shifters and Dragon Knights.

But as she thought of little Daisy and Freddie, and the children being friends despite all the odds against it, Ivy wanted to believe there was a better future for everyone. One that didn't include so much death, drugs, and destruction.

This is it. This was the tipping point, the one she couldn't return from if she went forward.

Would she keep holding on to what the Knights had taught her? Or, would she try to have a more open mind and believe what she saw with her own eyes?

There was only one real path at this point, and Ivy made her decision. However, she risked asking for a few things to see if she could get them. "I want to meet your mate and daughter, as well as the other humans living on Stonefire so I can talk with them. Agree to that, and I'll help you."

Nikki could've brushed her off, but the dragonwoman shrugged. "They'll want to meet you anyway, so I don't see why we can't arrange it."

It seemed almost too easy, but she kept her doubts to herself. "Okay then." Ivy raised her hand and gripped Nikki's. After a few pumps of their arms, Nikki released her hand and said, "I'll go get all the supplies waiting for you in the hall so we can get to work."

Nikki raced out of the room, and Jane said, "You made the right choice, Ivy. I hope you hold up your end of the bargain."

She bobbed her head but secretly hoped she could, too. Even though Ivy wanted to get over her fears and all the misinformation she'd been taught, it would take time. The only question was whether the dragon-shifters would be patient enough with her or grow frustrated, lock her in some cottage, and try to forget about her.

Or, in the worst-case scenario, they handed her over

to the DDA, and she never saw the sky again for the rest of her life.

But then Nikki raced back inside with her arms full of bags and boxes, and Ivy didn't have time to doubt or think about the future as the two women helped to make her feel human again.

Chapter Nine

Z ain stood inside a private waiting room and resisted pacing. Bram should've arrived by now to witness the mating ceremony. And since his clan leader was always on time, he worried a little.

His dragon spoke up. *This was put together at the last minute. And since he has three children and a mate at home, on top of the entire clan to care for, he's allowed to be a little late.*

Rationally, Zain knew this. But he wanted to start his assignment with Ivy as soon as possible.

His beast snorted. *Mating someone isn't really an assignment.*

It is to me. There are no feelings between us, and I have no intention of warming up to her. As I said before, we're not fucking her, ever.

Maybe. I don't fight you often, but when I do, I usually win. So you'd better hope I don't want the human or you won't stand a chance.

All the more reason for me to get the information I need as soon as possible. Once I have it, then I can focus my energy on finding her brother's killer or killers like I promised, which means not needing to be around the human any longer.

His dragon huffed, but his reply was cut off by Bram walking through the door.

Zain expected to see Kai and Jane right behind him, too, but Bram was alone. He shut the door and turned toward him. As the clan leader's blue eyes assessed him, he held his tongue. Bram had the hardest job inside the clan and had done much to improve the lives of everyone living on Stonefire. Zain held too much respect for the male to be demanding or grumpy like he was with almost everyone else.

Bram finally raised his brows. "Are you sure this is what you want? Just because Kai thinks it's the best option doesn't mean you have to agree to it."

Zain shook his head. "It's not just Kai's opinion that matters, Bram. The human talks more to me than anyone else, meaning I'm the best fit for her right now. I can protect her, watch her to determine if she's being sincere or playing us, and learn what she knows about our enemies. There's no downside to it."

Bram snorted. "Said by a male who's never been in love before."

Bram was one of a handful of loved-crazed males inside the clan now, which could be irritating on occasion. "I respect Evie like everyone else, and I'm glad you found her, but that sort of family life isn't for me, Bram. My strengths lie with protecting the clan. That's the future I want, nothing more."

"We'll see, Zain. We'll see." He opened his mouth to

protest more, but Bram beat him to it. "I won't keep trying to talk you out of it. However, I wouldn't be doing my job if I didn't at least ensure this is what you want, aye?" He nodded, and Bram continued, "Then let's go. Kai is on his way, Jane has the mating bands, and with Nikki, we'll have more than enough witnesses. Evie would've been here, too, but our youngest is fussing, and she didn't want to leave him."

They had two boys and one girl, all too young to even attend school yet. Zain didn't envy Bram and Evie at all.

His dragon grunted. *It wouldn't be so bad.*

Don't go hoping for children, dragon.

If we find our true mate, then your view won't matter.

Ignoring his beast, Zain followed Bram out of the private waiting area and down the corridor to Ivy's room.

Only to find Dr. Sid standing in front of Ivy's door, her arms crossed over her chest and a frown on her face.

His dragon whispered, *This isn't going to go well.*

As soon as they were close enough, Sid motioned with her head for them to follow her. Bram sighed. "Can't it wait, Sid?"

"No, but this won't take long. Let's go next door to talk. You, too, Zain."

Since no one on Stonefire crossed Sid, except for maybe her mate and Bram when she went too far, they followed. The instant the door closed, she spoke again. "Ivy has only started to regain her strength, and you want to force a mating ceremony on her? And no, don't try to say it's some kind of whirlwind romance, either, because that's bullshit."

Bram raised his brows. "It's not as if Zain's going to

jump her, Sid. This is for her safety as much as ours. Once the DDA learns she's here, I'll have no power over her fate unless she's mated to someone inside the clan."

His dragon murmured, *So he is thinking of the human female, too.*

Sid looked at Zain. "Swear here and now that you'll treat her as if she were your true mate, Zain. That means being nicer to her, not riling her up, and doing everything to ensure she recovers as quickly as possible. No matter what she's done in the past, she doesn't deserve a mate who'll only verbally and emotionally abuses her."

His dragon stood up and growled. Zain answered Sid before his beast could start shouting. "I can't be instantly nice to her, but I won't use her as a verbal punching bag, either."

Bram stepped in. "She'll be watched over, Sid. Ivy may be mating Zain, but Nikki and Jane have plans to visit her and introduce her to Mel and Evie. Maybe even to some of the children, too. She'll be treated well enough. I vow it."

Sid looked at Bram, then at Zain, and back again. "Fine, but you'll heed my medical advice concerning the human. She's still incredibly fragile and could relapse at any moment. At least until we find a permanent antidote for her. And yes, I'm working on that. Or, rather, Gregor is asking all the doctors who've joined our association of dragon doctors to help."

Zain grunted, not liking how the female doctor thought the worst of him. Did he really come off as such an arsehole to others? "I won't do anything to endanger her health. You have my word, Sid."

"Good." Sid motioned toward the door. "Then go and don't keep her waiting any longer."

Bram nodded at Sid in parting before exiting the room and entering the one beside it that was Ivy's. Zain followed his clan leader. However, as soon as Bram moved to the side, revealing the human female, Zain stopped in his tracks and blinked.

Gone was the pale, mussed-hair female. Ivy would always be pale, but the blue of her simple gown made her skin glow, and her ginger hair was piled atop her head with a few tendrils framing her face. However, instead of appearing more orange like before, her hair currently looked a deeper red.

If he didn't know anything about who she was or her past connections, he'd say she was beautiful.

His dragon growled. *Yes, she is. But I always knew that. You were just too blind to look. It's sad that she needs a hairstyle and different clothes to convince you she's pretty.*

Not wanting to encourage his beast, Zain ignored him and walked the remaining feet to her bed. Before he could think better of it, he muttered, "You look nice."

Wariness filled her gaze. "Er, thank you?"

Nikki snorted. "Don't be modest. You look fantastic, so own it."

Zain frowned at his fellow Protector. "You seem fairly chummy already."

Nikki shrugged. "We came to a sort of understanding. Maybe you should try it, too."

He was about to growl—Nikki was far too good at riling people up when she wanted—but Bram spoke before he could do so. "Enough. Let's get the ceremony started so I can go home and helped Evie with wee Gideon."

At the mention of Bram's youngest child, guilt flooded Zain's body. His clan leader was taking time away from his family to help Zain with his task. So he wouldn't delay it any longer. He asked, "Where are the mating bands?"

Jane held up a box. "Right here. But shouldn't we wait for Kai? He'll be here any second."

"There are a few things to do first, anyway, before we start." Bram motioned toward Ivy. "Has anyone explained how this works to you, Ivy?"

Ivy shrugged. "A little. But Nikki said Zain would go first, so I could just copy him when it comes to the wording of the mate vows."

Bram grunted. "Yes, that's true. Although, feel free to change the reasons why you're mating him to your own. Everyone in this room knows the truth anyway, so no need to lie."

Kai waltzed into the room and stopped at Jane's side. He leaned over to kiss his mate's cheek before speaking. "Let's hurry up. I need to get back to my final Protector assessment drills for Dacian."

Jane opened the box holding the mating bands and handed it to Bram. Once Stonefire's leader had it, he said, "Then let's begin."

Zain faced Ivy. A blush colored her cheeks, making her seem more alive than he'd seen since first discovering her unconscious in the woods. Her eyes in particular were bright and enticing.

And yes, if he didn't know her, he'd think she was

more than pretty—she was bloody beautiful.

However, this would be a mating of convenience, nothing more. Which meant he needed to stop noticing the deep blue of her eyes, or the redness of her lips.

His dragon huffed. *There's no reason to. With time, we could probably win her.*

No. Now hush, or I'll toss you into a mental prison.

Fine.

His dragon curled up into a ball but didn't go to sleep. A mating ceremony was a human need, but the dragon half recognized the importance and liked to witness it, too.

Zain picked up the slightly smaller silver band, one engraved with his name in the old dragon language. He slipped it onto Ivy's bicep—one that was too thin for his liking, because it reminded him of how uncertain her life was—and said, "Ivy Passmore, you were once our enemy, but you are slowly proving you're not anymore. I see potential in you, and intelligence. In exchange for your help, I will protect you with my life. Do you accept my claim?"

Not the most romantic of declarations, but then it wasn't supposed to be.

Ivy nodded. Bram then lowered the box so she could take the bigger band, the one engraved with her name in the old dragon language. He moved to give her better access to his bicep. As she slipped the band on, her fingers brushed his skin. Each tickle sent heat through his body, as well as a yearning for her to touch more than his arm.

Careful to keep his face expressionless, he didn't let on how she affected him.

He most definitely would need to keep his distance from her, or his cock might win out over his brain.

His inner beast laughed, but Zain didn't dignify him with a response.

Once the band was on his arm, he stood again, and Ivy spoke. "Zain Kinsella, when we first met, I fully expected you to kill me, torture me, or do any other number of things I was taught dragons did. However, you have slowly been helping me to understand your kind better. I hope this mating at least does that. Do you accept my claim?"

He wanted to snort at her wording but resisted. Honesty was better than her making up some pretend lies about feelings.

"Yes."

While not required, normally mating ceremonies ended with a kiss.

Zain's eyes darted to her lips, which looked fuller thanks to some sort of lip gloss.

His dragon hummed. *Yes, kiss her. Then maybe you won't hate her so much.*

No, I won't risk it.

Because there was always a slim chance that she was his true mate. And she wasn't strong enough for a frenzy.

Wait, what? There would be no frenzy. Ever. Not only because he wouldn't kiss her lips, but because fate wouldn't be that fucked up.

Not wanting to dwell on his slipup, Zain leaned over and kissed her cheek.

Which turned out to be a mistake. Her soft, warm skin was bad enough, but the faint scent of female and flowers filled his nose, making him want to lean closer and take a deeper inhale.

As if he were burned, Zain stood upright as quickly as possible and looked to Bram. "What about the paperwork?"

He snorted. "This is probably the first time someone has thought of the bloody DDA paperwork so quickly after mating a human." Zain merely raised his brows, and Bram sighed. "Fine, fine. My assistant is still working on it since this was put together so quickly. But once my assistant is finished, he'll bring it over. In the meantime, you stay here with your mate. A little surprise from all of us will arrive shortly, and you need to ensure you take care of Ivy."

He studied Bram closely but couldn't glean any extra information from his expression. "What's with the cryptic statement?"

Nikki grinned. "It's called a surprise, Zain."

"I don't like surprises," he muttered.

Ivy smiled—the first real smile he'd seen—and he stopped breathing a second. The human looked years younger, and less like an enemy, when she smiled.

Combined with her hair up and her blue dress, she was going to be a bigger threat to him than he'd thought. And Zain had only been mated to her for a few minutes.

His dragon laughed but said nothing. Probably because he didn't want to scare the human with flashing dragon eyes.

Still smiling, Ivy said, "It's been so long since I had a good surprise that I can't wait."

Of course she'd want surprises, although it made zero sense to Zain. Her last big surprise has been her brother's murder.

And just like that, Zain remembered why he'd mated Ivy and how things would be. No more noticing how pretty she was or thinking he wanted her to smile more often. No, he would protect her and work with her, nothing else.

He expected his dragon to say something, but he merely remained silent. And that made Zain more nervous than anything else.

Chapter Ten

Ivy had expected the mating ceremony to be solemn and perfunctory. And while her vows hadn't been the stuff people dreamed of, the aftermath had been quite nice.

First, feeling Zain's muscles underneath her fingers had sent a thrill of excitement through her body. Not to mention the kiss on her cheek made her blush furiously, as well as woke up certain lady parts she hadn't thought would ever respond to a dragon-shifter's touch.

But then Zain had moved away from her as quickly as possible, and the spell broke, reminding her this wasn't some sort of fairy tale. She was a human, he was a dragon-shifter, and there was a mile-wide ravine of hatred and fear between them.

However, Nikki's mention of a surprise garnered her full attention. Holidays hadn't been celebrated inside the Dragon Knights. After all, dragons didn't stop existing for a birthday or Christmas. And while she'd tried her best not to wish to have those things again— they'd been some of her favorite times of year before joining the Knights—it'd been hard not to have a tree to decorate or experience the anticipation of opening a present.

But her past was that—the past. Ivy needed to start celebrating the small things, such as surprises.

Bram shook her hand, smiled at her—was it real, she wondered—and left. And without thinking, Ivy turned toward Nikki. "Can't you give me a hint about what's coming?"

Nikki laughed. "Wow, if I'd known something as simple as a surprise would bring out the true Ivy hidden beneath all that fear and misinformation, I would've suggested it earlier."

The words stung a little, but Ivy wouldn't let them ruin the first real enjoyment she'd had in a long, long time. "That's still not a hint."

Jane snorted. "Tenacious, aren't you? Maybe with time, you'll fit in here nicely."

Not wanting to go down the road of thinking about her distant future, Ivy chanced a glance at Zain. The furrow of his brows made her blink. "Now what are you angry about?"

He grunted. "I don't like surprises."

And without thinking, she blurted, "Good, then there's more for me."

His frown deepened, and Ivy had no idea why. If they were to act as mates, he was bound to see more of her true self going forward.

Strange how a marriage of convenience had encouraged some of the old Ivy, the person she'd been before she'd joined the Knights, to come out of retirement.

No, it wasn't the fact she was now legally bound to a dragon-shifter that'd done it. The mention of a surprise had been the only reason. Yes, that was it.

A knock on the door made her heart rate kick up. What she wouldn't give to get out of bed and go see what was waiting on the other side.

However, it'd taken both Nikki and Jane's help to change her clothes earlier. Ivy had a long road of recovery still.

But as a pale, dark-haired woman walked through the door, pushing a wheelchair into the room, Ivy wasn't sure what to say. If that was her surprise, then she'd grossly overestimated it.

Nikki waved to the woman. "This is Dr. Emily Davies. She's a human, like you, and has been helping our doctors here on Stonefire. She convinced the other doctors to allow you a short visit outside the surgery, provided Emily's there to monitor you and that you're also in a wheelchair."

Zain growled before Ivy could say a word. "No. Taking her from the room is bound to send her into a relapse."

Emily raised her brows, her Welsh accent filling the room. "Just because I spend the majority of my time doing research doesn't make me less of a medical doctor. I know humans better than any other doctor here, Zain. Or, do you want to challenge me on that?"

Before anyone else could jump in, Ivy blurted, "Why is a human doctor living on Stonefire?"

Emily smiled at her. "That's a long story, and one I'll save for another day. We only have about an hour before I have to bring you back here. And considering it's sunny right now, we should take advantage of the weather before it changes its mind. Because I know that if I had been in a coma for so long, I'd want to feel the sun on my face again."

Nikki tossed back the blanket around Ivy's feet. "Come on. She's right, and we outnumber Zain four to one anyway. He can't win against us."

Zain muttered, "I'm her mate. Or did everyone just forget what happened here?"

Sensing this was a sort of test and would determine how their fake marriage would play out, she looked at Zain and stated, "The doctors have cleared the visit, so I'm going. Unless you're going to physically restrain me to the bed, then stop wasting what little time I can have out of this room."

Nikki grinned. "I bet Zain has ideas of how to restrain you to the bed."

Blood rushed to Ivy's cheeks as a mental image of Zain lying on top of her, his face mere inches from hers, flashed into her mind.

No. She could barely sit up by herself. Ivy wasn't going to think of sex.

Let alone sex with a dragon, of all things.

And especially not a grumpy, verbally stunted one at that.

Zain stepped back and waved toward the wheelchair. "Then risk your health. But no one can blame me if she dies. I'm entrusting her into your care, Nikki, meaning she's your responsibility until I get back."

With that, Zain stormed out of the room.

Jane looked toward the ceiling. "Overdramatic Zain is not the best side of him."

While she yearned to ask what *was* the best side of him, she let it drop for the moment since Emily positioned the wheelchair next to her bed and motioned for Nikki to help her.

Emily nodded toward the chair. "Okay, let's get you situated and go. We have a very important appointment with a sizable group of people we can't be late for."

Since it took everything she had just to move what little she could when Nikki and Emily asked her to, Ivy kept her questions to herself.

"A sizable group of people" seemed like a lot. Especially when it came to those who didn't outright hate her or wanted to hand her over to the DDA.

It seemed the full breadth of her surprise wasn't over.

But odd as it was, she was starting to trust Nikki. She and Ivy were about the same age, and the dragonwoman always just seemed so happy.

Could she ever be the same?

Not wanting to ruin what small amount of time she had out of her blasted hospital room, Ivy pushed every negative thought and doubt out of her head. After all, if someone from within Stonefire was going to hurt her, they would've done it while she was sleeping.

So after the women tucked a blanket around Ivy's lower body, as well as placed a light coat on her upper body, the doctor wheeled her out of the surgery. As they rolled along, Ivy forced herself to look ahead and not at the ground. She had a lot to be ashamed of in her past, but she needed to be strong when facing the dragons.

Or, so Nikki and Jane had mentioned to her.

Although when they entered the corridor, she realized her small show of bravery was wasted—it was empty. But as soon as they wheeled her out a back door and into the afternoon sunshine, she forgot all about it and instantly tilted her face upward, reveling in the heat on her skin.

She did that until the others cleared their throats, and Ivy opened her eyes. She spotted some clan members walking around, about ten or fifteen feet away.

One in particular caught her attention—a dark-haired male holding a small baby glared at her. Nikki stuck out her tongue at him and said, "That's my mate, Rafe, and our daughter. Ignore him. He thinks you have some master plan to kill me when I'm not looking."

Ivy watched the man as they wheeled past. He was tall and muscled, and it was hard to tell he was human and not a dragon-shifter. "I can barely sit up in this wheelchair. So unless I can kill things with my mind, you're safe."

Nikki laughed. "I think taking you out of the surgery was a good choice. Because if this is the real you, we will get along famously."

Was it her, though? For more than five years, she'd pushed her personality deep down, trying her best to hide it so she could focus on her work, determined to rise through the ranks of the Dragon Knights.

She had no idea who Ivy Passmore would be going forward.

Maybe sessions with Serafina Rossi would help her figure it all out.

Jane pointed toward a large brick building as they went past it. "That's where the security building is. In case you're curious about where Zain spends a lot of his time."

The building didn't stand out from most every other brick building in the country. But then a dragon jumped up from behind it and pumped its wings as it ascended into the sky, reminding her this was dragon territory.

Her first instinct was to huddle down and try to hide.

But Emily placed a hand on her shoulder and murmured, "Don't worry. That's Zain. He won't hurt you."

Finding out it was her dragonman, Ivy studied the deep red dragon. He was big, and his wings had to be extremely powerful as he effortlessly moved higher into the atmosphere. When the sun glinted over his hide, the red also revealed flecks of gold.

For the first time since she could remember, she thought a dragon was beautiful and not scary and abhorrent.

She truly was past the line of no return in her life. Unless she was personally attacked or threatened, Ivy didn't think she'd ever be deathly afraid of dragons again, let alone hate them.

Ivy watched until he disappeared into the horizon. "I guess he really wanted to get away from me for a bit, especially considering Bram told him to watch over me."

Jane was the first to speak. "Maybe, but not for the reasons you think. Besides, he trusts us to take care of you. Or, more importantly, Bram does and won't chew him out for it."

Nikki muttered, "It's still a little odd. I can barely get Rafe to trust others with our daughter, let alone me."

Jane replied, "I have a few tips I haven't shared yet on how to manage my brother. I'll share them later."

So Rafe was Jane's brother. That had to be the connection, the way Rafe had been allowed near female dragon-shifters in the first place before mating one.

As Ivy listened to the pair, it was clear they still didn't trust her as they spoke in vague statements. Not that she could blame them, but she desperately wanted to belong somewhere on this clan. And with more than a psychologist whose duty was to help her.

Which meant Ivy would just have to try to win over the children, starting with Freddie and Daisy. If she could manage that, then maybe the adults would give her a chance, or at least not outright despise her. Either way, she'd take what she could get.

As she tried to think of how to accomplish those goals, two familiar children rushed toward her—Freddie and Daisy.

Daisy ran faster and reached her first. "Hiya, Miss Passmore! We're your official guides for the day."

"Guides?" she echoed.

Daisy bobbed her head. "Yes. You're coming school for a bit. And I wanted to make sure you had some friends to answer questions before facing all the other students."

So the group the others had hinted about turned out to be an entire school. *Bloody brilliant.* Ivy hoped she had the energy to face them, especially since children rarely had filters and could be brutally honest.

And while she knew she'd have to face the truth eventually, maybe she wasn't ready to face it quite so head-on yet.

Freddie sighed and muttered something Ivy couldn't hear. No doubt, something unflattering.

However, Daisy didn't seem to notice. "Freddie will help me and you. He promised and knows how important promises are to me. Now, let's hurry up. Everyone's waiting. And we don't want Mr. MacLeod or Miss Lawson to get mad because we're late."

Emily gently squeezed her shoulder. "Don't worry about the students. They're just curious. And facing the questions you know are coming from children is easier than from adults, don't you think?"

"Maybe," she murmured.

Daisy took her hand and tugged, her wheelchair only staying put because of Emily's hold on it. "Come on. My class leaves Stonefire this afternoon. It's only a short visit, you know, to get ready for our play. So if you want some time with us, to see what we're doing, you have to hurry."

All eyes looked at her. Ivy doubted saying no would mean going back to the surgery. Still, she appreciated that they waited for her reply.

Again, their behavior was at odds with everything she'd been shown and taught for years.

Hoping she made the right choice, she nodded. "Okay, then let's go."

Letting go of Ivy's hand, Daisy jumped up and down a few times. "Yay! Everyone will be curious and have questions. Me, too. I have heaps. But I don't know if Mr. MacLeod will let me ask them all. He usually only allows one or two so that everyone else can have a chance. But I always have more than one or two. There's just so much to learn on Stonefire."

Freddie motioned with his hand. "Come on, Daisy. Or Miss Passmore won't have any time with our class at all, and no one's questions will get answered."

Daisy bobbed her head. "You're right, I guess. Let's go!"

Daisy raced ahead with Freddie.

Nikki murmured, "He's going to have his hands full in about four or five more years."

Ivy frowned. "What are you talking about?"

Emily pushed the wheelchair, and they all moved again. The doctor said, "Everyone on Stonefire is taking bets on them being true mates or not. They're far too young, of course—they're nearly eleven. And dragons don't fully mature until age twenty. However, Freddie is one of the few who can get Daisy to focus or stop talking. But who knows if that will be the case when they're teenagers."

Ivy studied the quickly disappearing pair. She couldn't keep from asking, "Were the classes introduced that way on purpose? To pair up humans and dragons?"

Jane sighed. "Who would ask that? Oh, right, a former Dragon Knight. No, it was merely for the children to get to know one another and hopefully make friends."

"Oh," she stated. Without being surrounded by hate and bias, it made sense. If dragons and humans interacted from the time they were children, they'd be more familiar and at ease when they were adults.

Ivy hoped the Knights hadn't got wind of Stonefire's efforts with the schoolchildren. Otherwise, they could become targets, too.

Just something else she needed to share when she had the chance.

Jane placed a hand on her hip. "You know what? The more we learn from you, the more horrible the Knights sound. Did they also say humans offer up virgins to appease the dragons?"

Ivy bit her lip. While the idea had seemed plausible when she was younger, it sounded a bit ridiculous now. "Yes. That was some of the rationale behind creating the Dragon Knights centuries ago. They wanted to show they could protect humans from the dragons, so it was better to hire them to slay the beasts than to keep appeasing the dragons with offerings."

Jane grunted. "So they were mercenaries pretending to be righteous. Why does that not surprise me?"

Emily chimed in. "Relations have changed over the decades, sometimes for the better and sometimes for the worse. But it's our job to create our own future, right?"

"Says the female who doesn't go after what she wants herself," Nikki said with a sly look on her face.

Ivy glanced between the pair. "What are you talking about?"

Emily shook her head. "Yet another story for a different time. The school is straight ahead of us. Some of the other students should rush out to meet you any second now."

The human doctor had a lot of stories and secrets. Not that Ivy could prod more since Freddie and Daisy rushed out of the building, Daisy holding the hand of another student her age with black hair. Even from about ten feet away, Ivy could hear Daisy say, "See, Emily? I told you today would be brilliant. Not only is Nikki here —I wish I could shift into a dragon and be a Protector, too—the other Emily came, as well as the lady who's been asleep for a year inside the surgery. This is so much better than painting sets for the play, right?"

The little girl said something Ivy couldn't hear, but she soon forgot all about the children as a tall, dark-haired man with a tattoo on his bicep came out. Nikki whispered, "That's Tristan MacLeod, one of the teachers. He's the mate of the female who wrote the famous book about dragon-shifters."

So, the dark-haired man with narrowed eyes was mated to Melanie Hall.

Who had been, and probably still was, one of the top targets of the Knights. Anyone who steered public opinion in favor of the dragon-shifters was a top priority.

Ivy blurted, "I hope she's protected."

Nikki and Jane both faced her. "Why?"

She hesitated a second at Nikki's flashing pupils, but finally managed to reply, "She's been one of the Dragon Knights' top targets for years. Her name, and others, are on an encrypted file inside the information I brought with me."

Jane shook her head. "I told you we should've arranged a meeting with Nate and Lucien instead of this."

Emily cleared her throat. "No, this is better for her mental health, and we're sticking to the plan."

Nikki raised her brows as she stared at Ivy. "Before you fall asleep again, you're going to tell us what file you're talking about as well as how to unlock it."

She bobbed her head, and Nikki relaxed a fraction. The dragonwoman gestured toward the school. "The kids are all but dancing and asking a chorus of 'Why aren't they moving?' Let's get a move on, or Tristan really will be in a bad mood."

Not wanting to see any dragon-shifter in a bad mood, Ivy motioned with her hand. "Then let's go. I don't have a lot of time before we have to get back. I can give you all the necessary information once we return to the surgery."

As Emily wheeled her toward the students standing in front of the school, Ivy took a few deep breaths. Her time with the children could tell her a lot about the weeks, months, or even years she'd spend on Stonefire. And considering she'd mated Zain, she had a feeling Stonefire would be her future for some time to come.

The only question was whether she'd always be seen as an enemy, or could she try to make amends and fit in?

Trying not to think of how far she'd come in nearly two weeks, Ivy did her best to hide her fear at the flashing dragon eyes among half the children, and forced a smile.

Chapter Eleven

Zain glided back toward Stonefire, wishing he had another village or farm to visit.

His dragon grunted. *Stop coming up with excuses. We mated Ivy today, and instead of getting to know her, you're doing everything you can to stay away from her.*

Of course I bloody am. You're too calm around her and don't recognize the danger. Her blushes were bright warning signals to keep my distance for a bit. I'm not going to encourage anything with her.

But wasn't the point of mating her so that you could spend time around her, to get information? Not to mention regardless of how you feel about Ivy, she's ours to protect now.

Yes, that was true, she was. But Zain trusted Nikki to look after her for a bit.

Not to mention he needed the distance, too. It took every iota of cleverness he possessed to keep his reactions to Ivy secret from his inner beast.

When he wasn't careful, the feel of her soft cheek under his lips would flash into his mind. A cheek that was also warm and begged to nuzzle against his own. Not to mention her scent had surrounded him, stoking his desire to strip her and claim her properly.

Thank goodness for his iron-clad control, or no doubt his cock would've joined the party, letting everyone in the room know he wanted the human for more than a source of information.

And not just any human, but one of his fucking enemies. Sure, she was a *former* enemy, but that didn't make much difference to him.

At least his dragon hadn't picked up on Zain's thoughts during the ceremony. Otherwise, his dragon would play the memory of them kissing her cheek on a loop, hoping to wear Zain down enough to at least give the female a chance.

As if he ever could.

Right?

To avoid thinking about that thought, Zain replied to his beast, *And we will protect the human, of course we will. As soon as we land back on Stonefire, we'll look for her, okay?*

His beast huffed. *You better. I want to see her in that dress again, before they put her back into a hospital gown.*

The vivid blue dress that had made her skin glow.

No, Zain needed to purge thoughts like that. Ivy may be trying to help them for the time being, but in his book, she would always be his enemy first and everything else after.

His dragon growled, meaning Zain hadn't kept his

last few thoughts private. *Usually you're more openminded about people. Give her a chance.*

If she earns it, then maybe. But I won't risk the clan. All too easily she could turn and show her true colors again, hurting many of the people we love. Do you really want to put Freddie or Alfie in danger?

Don't use our nephews as a shield for what you don't want to recognize.

Which is?

That Ivy may have decided to help us and is accepting the truth before her.

What his dragon didn't say was more important—if she did accept the truth and helped them eradicate the Knights, Zain would have fewer excuses to keep away from the female he'd mated.

He mentally sighed, wishing his life was a little easier. *There's the landing area. The quicker we touch ground, the quicker we can go find her. That should make you happy.*

Fine, be grumpy. I'll enjoy the human for us both.

Not wanting to read into his beast's words, Zain allowed his dragon to maneuver them toward the landing area and to slowly touch the ground again. Within seconds, his snout shrunk into a nose, his wings retreated into his back, and his limbs returned to normal size.

After quickly pulling on his clothes, Zain headed toward the school and checked his mobile phone, finding a few messages. According to Nikki's text message, they were in the school's auditorium and would be there for an hour or two. Since the timestamp was nearly two hours ago—with no follow-up note from Nikki about a change of plans—part of him wondered if he lucked out and would only have to deal with Ivy inside her hospital room again.

For some reason, when she was in that bed and wearing her hospital garb, he could think clearer. He might be able to avoid the pretty blue dress that made him forget she'd been his enemy in the past.

Zain reached the school grounds, waved to some of the staff outside the auditorium, and entered.

The room was large, with seats around the edges that could be folded up against the wall. Unlike most human ones he'd seen in pictures, the Stonefire school had a retractable ceiling. After all, it helped to have dragons land right in the room instead of having them shift in front of the students. Some of the young ones would get ideas about how to attempt to shift on their own, which was never good with an untrained dragon out to prove themselves.

Students, and quite a few parents, filled the seats. He also noted a few clan members who weren't teachers, including Blake Whitby—the dragonman helping with the special effects for the kids' play—and a teenage human boy named Oliver, who was Melanie Hall-MacLeod's younger brother.

So the meeting was for more than just the students, then.

Zain visually searched through the crowd for Ivy and finally found her sitting off to the side in a wheelchair. A long queue started at her location and wound around the empty and open center of the room.

Keeping close to the wall, mostly hidden by one of the stands, Zain watched Ivy as she spoke with one child and then another.

She mostly smiled and nodded. And while he noted the dark circles under her eyes, meaning she had to be tired, she looked more alive and animated than he'd seen her so far.

And the students who talked with her didn't look angry. No, many of them had wide eyes and slack jaws, as if in awe of the human female.

It seemed Ivy had won over some of the children in less than two hours. She was either really good at playing people, or she had a natural affinity for children.

His dragon spoke up. *Then why not give her a child? She won't get one from anyone else anytime soon. And then I will have someone to pass on my knowledge and skills to.*

No, we're not talking about babies right now.

His beast huffed. *And people think I'm the stubborn half.*

A familiar voice came from his right—Bram's. "You finally showed up, I see."

Zain never took his gaze from Ivy's form, watching her every move to determine her tells. "I had some duties to attend to. Nikki and Jane watched over her for me, and since you trust them, too, I don't see the problem."

Bram kept his voice low so that only Zain could hear him. "If you weren't going to act as her mate, then you shouldn't have claimed her."

He finally met Bram's gaze. "Not even you spend every second of every day with Evie."

Bram raised his brows. "No, but I bloody well tried

for the first few months and still do, if I can manage it. And before you say ours is a love match, just know that not all matings start out that way, especially with some true mates."

Zain shook his head. "I don't think she's mine. But regardless, give me a detailed list of what I need to do to satisfy your standards, and I'll meet them."

Bram grunted. "Surliness isn't helping you, Zain. Stop taking your mood out on me and go talk with the lass."

He could deny that he couldn't care less about talking with Ivy unless she was going to impart information related to the Dragon Knights.

Yet as he watched her smile and sometimes high-five or fist-bump a student, a thread of something unfamiliar wound through his body.

He refused to call it jealousy. No, Zain merely felt bound to fulfill his mate duties.

He finally muttered, "Fine, I'll go watch over her. Will that make you happy?"

"For now."

Before Bram could delve into a lecture or some sort of sage advice, Zain crossed the length of the room until he stood next to Ivy in her wheelchair. He couldn't help but noticed her flushed cheeks and the glint in her eye he hadn't seen before—one of excitement.

She was having fun.

His dragon growled. *We could've brought that light out if you'd tried a little.*

Ignoring his beast, he waited for the latest child—who kept stuttering—to finish before he leaned down and whispered into Ivy's ear, "Tell me the truth—are you tired?"

She moved her head and her hair brushed against his lips.

Her hair was far softer than it should be.

Before he could do something stupid, such as kiss her head and take a deep inhale of her scent, he moved back until he could see Ivy frowning at him. She replied, "I didn't know you were back. But yes, I'm fine. Emily keeps checking me out every five minutes or so, just to make sure."

"But it's been longer than an hour, and that's how long you were approved for."

Ivy raised her brows. "I have Emily's blessing to remain here." She lowered her voice to the smallest whisper. "Besides, they're being nicer to me than you ever were. Excuse me whilst I enjoy not being overly hated for a bit longer."

His dragon stood and stretched his wings. *You should be nicer to her, too.*

A little boy Zain recognized as Elliott Wells tugged on Ivy's sleeve to get her attention.

She turned and smiled at the little boy. When he smiled back, Zain resisted frowning again.

Elliott's mother, Charlie, had been killed by dragon hunters. While they were a separate group from the Knights, they were just as brutal and determined to harm dragon-shifters.

How could Elliott's father let him interact so freely with an enemy, even if she was a former one?

His dragon spoke up. *Hudson works on some IT jobs with*

Lucien. He would know about Ivy's thumb drive full of informa-tion, and that might be enough for the male to give her a chance.

Everyone kept talking about giving Ivy a bloody chance, ignoring everything she did in the past. However, before he could share his frustration with his dragon, Daisy ran toward him and shouted, "Uncle Zain!"

He'd long ago stopped trying to tell her he wasn't her uncle. When Daisy skidded to a halt next to him, she tugged his sleeve. "You're not taking Ivy away yet, are you? I promised her a sneak peek at the sets for our play. And she mentioned knowing some science stuff, so maybe she could help with the special effects. Mr. Whitby keeps trying to find the perfect controlled explosion. Something about not wanting to catch everyone on fire, so a fake one. But a good one, of course."

Zain opened his mouth to reply, but Daisy turned toward Ivy and continued on, "You're staying a little longer, right, Miss Passmore? We can go see the sets and talk with Mr. Whitby right now. I know the other kids will be disappointed at you leaving, but you already said you'd come back to the Stonefire school again. So they can save their questions for later. The sets and play won't be there for much longer, only until we put on the show. After that, they'll probably be stored again. And if Mr. Whitby doesn't figure out his special extra for us, then the play won't be as good. You need to help him."

Good thing Daisy was not quite eleven years old. If she were an adult, Zain might be afraid of what her forceful personality would do to his clan.

His dragon snorted. *She loves dragons too much to hurt us.*

Just because she loves us doesn't mean she won't do something unintentional to harm us.

Ivy's reply interrupted his conversation with his beast. "I think that's a good idea, Daisy. I need to leave soon so I can rest anyway. And I do want to try and help Mr. Whitby if I can."

Daisy jumped. "Yes! Okay, I'll go get him and let him know." Daisy looked up at Zain. "Make sure she comes to the storage room where we're doing sets and things. If you scowl at anyone who tries to talk with Miss Passmore on the way, then it'll scare the other students off. So make sure to scowl a lot."

With that, the curly-haired human rushed off.

Ivy spoke softly, her voice full of humor. "I rather like Daisy."

"I'm glad someone does," he muttered half-heartedly. He was secretly fond of his nephew's friend and didn't mind her calling him uncle, but someone would have to rip off his fingernails before he'd admit it. "Should I clear us visiting the other room for a bit with the doctor then?"

She blinked up at him. "You're going to take me?"

"I *am* your mate. Besides, I've kept Nikki away from her daughter long enough. And I can't let Daisy down, either."

Ivy glanced over her shoulder, and Zain did his best not to notice her long, graceful neck. Or how twisting her body exposed a little of her cleavage in the neckline of her dress.

No. He wasn't going to notice. Especially since they'd be spending a lot of time alone together in the future.

And if he kept noticing her body, his cock may take over his brain and make him do something stupid.

His dragon mumbled something incoherently and settled down to the back of their mind. For once, his dragon wasn't going to berate or argue.

While there was most definitely some ulterior motive behind it, Zain pushed aside the niggle of curiosity. Without another word, he strode over to Nikki, Jane, and Emily, who all stood together. Nikki tilted her head and smiled. "Come to finally claim your mate?"

"Not claim, but accompany. I'll take over her guard duty for now."

The human doctor spoke up. "She can't stay out much longer, Zain. She needs to be back at the surgery within the next half hour, or she could possibly relapse."

He grunted. "I promise she'll be back by then. With me standing over her, I'll be able to get her in and out of the set room rather quickly."

Jane snorted. "Unless Daisy wants her to stay."

"I can handle a little human girl."

Jane replied, "We'll see. She has that talent of being able to wrap males around her little finger."

Not wanting to waste any more time, Zain turned and headed back to Ivy. She said farewell to one last student before looking up at him. "Where's Emily? Shouldn't she come with us, too?"

"You're in my care for the next thirty minutes. That's how much time we have between now and you being helped back into your bed. I'll start the time now."

Ivy snorted. "Someone sounds a bit cocky. If I had a stopwatch, I'd time you."

He blinked. Was the human teasing him? "Well, you don't. But I'm rather good with keeping time. So let's go, and I'll let you know when it's time to head back to your room."

He pushed the wheelchair slowly, the kids moving out of the way. And if they didn't, he merely growled and lifted his brows, and they scurried away.

Sometimes it was good to have a reputation as a scary Protector.

His dragon yawned. *Not scary. Maybe a little intimidating, but nothing else.*

I thought you were taking a nap?

I am. Maybe if you spend time alone with Ivy, without me nagging you, then you'll see more of what I see.

Which is?

Figure it out yourself.

His beast curled up, tucked his head under his tail, and closed his eyes. Even if he were faking it, his dragon wouldn't say anything until he was ready.

Once they were out of the auditorium and in an empty hallway, Ivy stated, "I enjoyed today. Maybe if I stayed here, I could be a teacher or teacher's assistant eventually."

Before he could think otherwise, he spat, "If the parents could forgive you for your past."

The second the words left his lips, he mentally cursed. He'd vowed not to use her as a verbal punching bag. "Ivy, I—"

"Save it, Zain. Not even you being an arsehole can take away the last few hours from me."

Mated less than a day, and his mate thought him an arsehole.

It shouldn't matter to him, it really shouldn't. The mating was fake. His duty was only to protect her, nothing else.

And yet, the thought of her hate festering didn't sit well with him. He needed to do better. And fast.

He continued to wheel her down the corridor to the correct room and searched his brain for how to be a decent mate to Ivy and stop treating her like crap. Otherwise she'd never tell him anything.

And yes, that had to be the real reason for his regret. He was too scared to think of any other cause.

Ivy's NERVOUSNESS had faded quickly with the school children. True, some asked difficult questions about why she was there or if she had any family. Not to mention more than a few hovered at the edges of the room, wanting nothing to do with her. However, those who'd queued up to talk with her had made her day.

Well, more like her year considering she'd been unconscious for nearly that long.

All of the questions, plus Nikki joking with some of the students about Ivy, had lowered her guard. It was almost impossible for her to believe an entire school had coordinated to trick her.

Which meant her last major doubts about the dragons being the monsters she'd been taught they were faded.

No, she wouldn't trust just anyone. But she could at least look around, observe, and judge for herself.

Dr. Rossi would probably have some fancy words for that realization.

Zain stopped in front of a door and grunted. "We're here. Are you sure you're not too tired?"

"Why, afraid they won't allow me in the same room as the students? Being an enclosed area and all, I could pick them off one by one," she drawled.

"No, you have dark circles under your eyes and you look haggard. That's why."

Zain visibly winced at his words. Could it be regret?

No, he'd made it clear that he didn't like her. Which was fine, but she wasn't about to let him ruin her day. "Well, this haggard human can handle looking over some notes and discussing chemistry with another being who understands it."

He searched her eyes a second before he said, "Before we go in, let me say this—I don't purposely try to be mean to you. It just happens."

She shook her head. "I'm not sure that makes it any better. After all, if I can try to shift my entire world view about your kind, you can at least try to be nice to one human."

The words surprised even Ivy, but she wasn't going to apologize for them. Jane, Emily, and Nikki had all repeated how she needed to stand up to Zain. And while there was zero chance of anything romantic happening between them—his hatred was too great—she could put the dragonman in his place a few times if it meant he'd be nicer to her.

His pupils flashed, reminding her of the beautiful red dragon ascending into the sky and an idea formed. "And you can start by letting me a have a private viewing of your dragon once I've rested and can go out again. I need to practice not flinching or showing fear, and it'll make you learn restraint because I'm fairly certain your clan leader wouldn't like you eating me as a snack."

He cleared his throat. "We don't eat humans. Cows or deer are much tastier to our dragon forms. And before you go off about us stealing them, we have our own farms stocked with those beasts, and more."

Interesting. That was something the Dragon Knights had never mentioned to her. Although she had to admit, it was hard to picture a dragon farmer or rancher. "So do you agree to the private session? Or, will you turn that down and run away again?"

"I didn't run away," he muttered.

She fought a smile. He *had* run from her earlier. The question was why, given he'd spent so much time trying to be in her room with her before.

He sighed and nodded. "Okay, fine. Once the doctors approve another outing, I'll show you my dragon form. But at the first sign of fear, I'm changing back. I promised to look after you, and that includes not sending you into a relapse or back into another coma."

She mustered up enough energy to raise a hand, offering to shake on it. Ivy fully expected for him to ignore it and turn away. But after a second, he took her hand in his and gently squeezed.

The warm, rough fingers from her first massage from him hadn't changed. And something about his hand dwarfing hers, almost as if it were shielding her hand from others, made her feel safe.

Then he turned her hand over and ran a finger back and forth across her inner wrist. Ivy couldn't contain her shiver at the light touch. She whispered, "What are you doing?"

His murmured, "Showing you that I can be gentle. I think from now on, I'll be doing your physical therapy again."

Images of Zain running his hand up her legs, to her thighs, and squeezing or pressing against her nearly made Ivy squirm in her seat. Him being nice was almost too much.

Add in his strong hands massaging her flesh day after day, and Ivy wasn't so sure mating Zain had been the best idea.

Because if he kept it up, she'd want something she couldn't have.

And not just because she craved closeness after so many years in near isolation with the Knights, either.

Before she could form words, he dropped her hand and opened the door, breaking the spell.

Inside the room, a few kids lingered with some paint sets. Toward the back, the dragonman with light brown hair and light skin she'd seen back inside the auditorium sat in front of a computer. It was Blake Whitby.

Right, it was time to focus on chemistry and other scientific knowledge. That would help her forget about Zain and his big, warm hands.

So as soon as he maneuvered her to the other drag-onman, she ignored Zain and focused on what made sense in her world—science—for as long as possible. The distraction was only temporary, but something about discussing facts, numbers, and hypotheses made her feel like her younger self, from a time before she'd joined the Dragon Knights.

Maybe that was the person she was supposed to be.

Chapter Twelve

Zain tried his best to moderate his pace and not full-on run as he made his way toward the clan's surgery to see Ivy again.

While he'd slept the night on a cot inside Ivy's room, she'd fallen asleep the day before, upon returning from the school, and hadn't woken up yet.

He'd been concerned, but the doctors assured him that she was merely sleeping, and he should do some of his Protector duties while he could.

So he had. However, her unconsciousness made him uneasy, and he was eager to check up on her again.

His dragon spoke up. *I told you we shouldn't have left her side.*

We had to check in with Kai, Lucien, and Nate.

The trio had sifted through the now-decoded data. And while they had some answers, the information had only prompted more questions. Kai left it up to him to decide when Ivy was strong enough to face them. No one wanted to trigger an unsavory memory and possibly turn her hysterical, or worse, cause a relapse.

Not that Zain suspected she would easily be triggered. A female who could find her brother murdered, devise a plan, and run into the arms of her enemy was stronger than most people gave credit to.

His dragon snorted. *Now who's defending her?*

Ignoring his dragon, he entered the back entrance to the surgery and headed straight for Dr. Sid and Gregor's shared office space. He knocked and entered once Sid told him to. He found the pair sitting in desks facing each other, mountains of paperwork everywhere.

Once Zain shut the door behind him, he asked without preamble, "How's Ivy?"

Gregor raised a dark blond eyebrow. "You were gone an hour, so nothing's changed. And if it had, we would've let you know."

Dr. Sid steepled her fingers in front of her. "If you're getting attached to her, Zain, then make sure you keep your cock in your pants until she's stronger."

He growled. "Careful, Sid."

Sid raised her hands, her palms facing toward him. "I will for now. But if it comes to that point, when you're thinking of having sex with her, you need to talk with us first. And not just to ensure she's healthy enough, either."

His irritation faded a fraction at Dr. Sid's cryptic statement. "What does that mean?"

Gregor answered, "It's possible the poison used on her had a biological element, one that could be transmitted through bodily fluids. Until we can rule it out for certain—her bloodwork has more mysteries than we like —be careful."

The fact the doctors knew so little about Ivy's situation made his dragon pace inside his head. *How are we supposed to protect her from that?*

We can't, he stated.

Zain spoke to the doctors again. He grunted. "I'm not thinking of tossing her over a chair and fucking her. All I want is to give her some physical therapy and take her out to see my dragon when she's strong enough. Can I do either today?"

Dr. Sid shrugged. "The PT will be fine. As for another excursion so soon after yesterday, you're going to have to wait. Maybe in a day or two, she can go out again for a couple hours, but no more."

A phone buzzed on Gregor's desk. After the dragonman checked it, he said to his mate, "Ivy's awake. All her signs are stable and seem good. For now."

His dragon stood a little taller at the mention of Ivy being awake. Zain tried not to notice it and said, "Right, then I'm going to see her. Let me know the second you have more information on her status, ailment, or whatever the fuck is wrong with her."

He strode from the room and headed for Ivy's. His dragon decided to chime in. *Well, if we can't sleep with her, then it gives you plenty of time to get to know her better.*

Not this again.

After he'd put Ivy back to bed the previous evening, he'd stared at her sleeping form for longer than he'd liked. Watching her interact with Blake had been fascinating.

Because while Zain's eyes would glaze over at the first talk of formulas, Ivy had become even more animated.

She truly had a love for science.

Maybe she could use that talent to better guard his clan and the other dragons around the world.

Of course, since she'd been so at ease with Blake, Zain had done his fair share of glaring. Not that the male seemed to notice Zain's glower, or even Ivy as a female.

Given how the shy male rarely interacted with other clan members and was teased as a hermit, it shouldn't really surprise Zain.

But how could someone not notice her lovely ginger hair or eyes that reminded him of the deep parts of the ocean?

His dragon laughed, but Zain ignored him. He was allowed to notice his mate's beauty, even if he had no intention of acting on it.

Liar, his beast muttered.

He reached Ivy's room, knocked, and entered without waiting for a reply—and caught sight of a nurse pulling the gown over Ivy's pale, naked back.

While Ivy needed to gain weight still, the long curve of her spine and the smooth skin dotted with freckles made him want to rush over and kiss each and every one of those little spots.

And continue his quest until he'd found every single one on her body.

No. Former Knight, former Knight, former Knight, he repeated inside his head. She could never be his. To do so would be a betrayal to his clan.

So Zain pushed aside every last erotic thought he had

of Ivy and waited for the nurse to finish. Then he strode over and sat on the edge of her bed. "I have some questions for you."

His beast sighed. *So much for easing into it.*

I have to do it this way.

Why?

Not deigning his dragon with an answer, Zain stared at Ivy and waited for her to react.

A NURSE HAD BEEN in the process of retying her hospital gown after the morning examination when a sizzle went down her spine. At first, Ivy wondered if it had something to do with her condition or even a sign she was on the road to recovery. However, when Zain appeared in front of her and sat on her bed, she instantly knew it'd been his eyes on her back that had heated her skin.

She'd seen many fit dragon-shifters the day before, but none of them elicited the same response as it did with Zain.

The man she had mated and would be spending lots of time with, but would never truly be hers.

Not that she wanted him that way. No, that would be ridiculous.

As Ivy struggled to come to terms with her body's responses, Zain stated in his growly voice, "I have some questions for you."

Nurse Ginny huffed and spoke before Ivy could. "You can wait another few minutes, Zain Kinsella. Ivy needs to eat her breakfast before doing anything else."

She expected Zain to argue, but he nodded, crossed his arms, and waited, never budging from his spot on her bed.

Great. She was going to have an audience for her bland meal.

Trying her best to ignore the hulk of a dragonman on her bed, Ivy allowed Ginny to spoon some of the special, barely warm soup concoction they forced her to eat every morning. Still, from the corner of her eye, she noticed Zain following the spoon to her lips, to the bowl, and back again.

It was on the tip of her tongue to ask him if he needed to document her eating habits to his boss, but didn't. The sooner she finished her food, the sooner Ginny would leave her alone.

And while during those first few days Ivy had feared being alone with Zain, she actually looked forward to it now. Mostly because she wanted to ask about seeing his dragon again, and to see if he kept his word about being nice to her. It would be fascinating to have an almost normal conversation with him.

"Almost" because it'd still be her talking with a dragon-shifter, something she still had trouble believing.

Once she finished the last of her food, Ginny raised her eyebrows at Zain as some kind of warning and left them alone.

Silence fell, but after a few beats, Zain said, "Are you ready now for some questions? Or do I need to brush your hair first, to finish you getting ready? Although I'll be honest—if I touch it, then it won't look much better than it is now."

His tone of voice was lighter, almost as if he were… teasing her. But that couldn't be true. Could it?

She answered, "This is about as good as I'll get today, I'm afraid. So, what questions do you have? Is it related to the data I brought with me? Did your team manage to decrypt it all?"

His eyes widened a fraction, and she resisted a smile. Good. She liked keeping him on his toes.

Zain cleared his throat, uncrossed his arms, and nodded. "Some of our scientists looked over the recently decrypted dragon-drug formulas and weapon schematics, but nothing's been found yet about an all-out attack on our kind. And we all think that's inevitable. So tell me—is a war coming that we need to know about?"

She shrugged. "If it hasn't happened in the year I've been unconscious, then I have no idea. The formulas are ways to keep dragons from shifting, and the schematics are for portable anti-dragon guns and lasers. The rumor was that the leaders wanted everything sorted and ready before truly attacking with force. It's why only small groups of dragon-shifters have been targeted over the last few years."

Zain grunted. "They were merely test subjects."

She nodded. "The random attacks by different factions within the Knights was to make the attacks appear unprofessional and scattered. In truth, there is a small group or council—we were never told the exact details about the organization at the top—that's plotting every step."

Zain searched her eyes. "But you were telling the truth before, about not knowing who they are?"

"Yes. Just like the different factions didn't all know the others were also testing drugs on dragon-shifters, most departments within the Knights never interacted with others unless absolutely necessary. So, for example, the research and technology departments never met with the regular foot soldiers, or even the accountants."

He frowned. "Then how did you steal all the data?"

She tilted her head. "That was an oversight, one they won't overlook again, I'm sure. Since I was in charge of the chemical research department, I demanded to see every bit of data we had on dragon-shifters. It's true that you can't devise new formulas or poisons to be more effective without all the knowledge available. However, rather than having access only to reports and general data collections, someone granted me full access. I didn't pay much attention to the other data at first. But eventually, as I learned about the children's kidnappings and testing, I started to feel uneasy. The more children they took, the worse the feeling grew until I knew I couldn't keep helping them."

"And so you copied as much of the data as you could and escaped," Zain stated.

She bobbed her head. "I had no idea there was another group of scientists creating the strange poison to keep us all hostage or I may not have had the courage to run. If I hadn't made it to Stonefire's lands when I did, then I would've been a sitting duck for them and easily dead by now." She glanced down at her blanket and plucked the material with her fingers. "I truly am sorry for the role I played in hurting any of the children here or elsewhere in the UK." Taking a deep breath, she met

Zain's gaze again. "I hope maybe this time you'll start to believe me."

He studied her face a second before he said softly, "I have no bloody idea why, but I do."

His words sent a thrill throughout her body, one that should worry her, but Ivy did her best to ignore. "Good. Then let me know what other information you need so I can help as much as possible."

"In a minute. First, I need to know something unrelated to the Knights, something personal."

As his eyes flashed, she murmured, "What?"

"There must've been some sort of fear or hatred lingering inside you before you encountered the Friends of the World. Where did it come from? Why were you afraid of us?"

Ivy blinked and tried to process his question. After a few beats, she replied quietly, "I don't know the exact moment. But parents tell stories before bedtime, about the dragon-shifters coming to get us if we were naughty. Plus, the only real history we're taught in school concerning dragon-shifters is about the human-dragon wars that have happened over the centuries." She shrugged one shoulder. "So I guess my only real knowledge about your kind was negative."

Zain watched her face as he said quietly, "So when someone offered you further proof of those views, you took to it."

"I'm not a therapist, but I suppose so." She paused a second before adding, "However, I think what you're doing with the school children now will help with that, by preventing the fear from growing."

Zain's lips twitched upward. It was the closest Ivy had ever seen him smile.

And it made him look entirely too humanlike.

Her heart thumped at the crack in his stony façade. Was there anyone who made him smile on a regular basis? Did he ever laugh?

However, before her mind went too far down that road, Zain spoke again. "I think the children getting together and having fun is easing everyone's fears a little here. There are still plenty of humans who refuse to allow their children to participate in any of the activities we've hosted for the kids. But those who have come here and joined in might help our reputations in the long run. Especially when combined with the effort of the other humans living here on Stonefire."

Aware the spell of honesty and almost ease between them could break at any second, Ivy decided to ask Zain a personal question. "You obviously have a mistrust of certain humans yourself. Why?"

He threaded his fingers together and sighed. "They brutally murdered one of my friends. Not to mention they've hurt so many others here and elsewhere in the UK. Just the thought of the hunters or Knights getting to my nephews is enough to make my dragon roar, as well as makes me itch to jump and fly away to find and eradicate every last threat to them."

As Ivy tried to think of how to respond to that—she was one of the former enemies after all—Zain continued, "But there's one more thing from my past, something that makes it harder for me to like adult humans more than most of the other dragon-shifters on Stonefire."

Ivy leaned forward a little. "What happened?"

Zain glanced down at his hands. The lowering of his alpha, impenetrable façade nearly made her blink. She hadn't really thought of him having vulnerabilities. Yes, he had loved ones, but the man himself seemed so strong.

But he had weaknesses just like everyone else.

Ivy tried not to read into how much sharing this with her meant. The only reason she could fathom he would think of it was to try and make their mating more amicable.

Zain grunted and said, "Every Protector has to serve two years with the British Army before they're given a final series of tests and allowed to join the security team on their clan. The male or female usually serves around age twenty or so, once a dragon-shifter is fully matured."

Yet another thing Ivy had never known before—dragons voluntarily served in the armed forces along with humans. The Knights had told them they were forced into service. "And since you're a Protector, you spent that time surrounded by humans, too. So I'm guessing someone hurt you during that time, or you wouldn't have brought it up."

He shrugged one shoulder. "Hurt is a vague word, but yes. My human superior lusted after me from the first day, and it didn't take long for him to let me know it, too. And whilst there are dragon males who prefer other males—or both males and females—I prefer females only. I told him so, and he didn't like it. So he threatened to kick me out of the army on some sort of violation unless I did as he asked."

She frowned. "But he didn't carry out his threat, right? Or you wouldn't be a Protector now. So what happened?"

Zain narrowed his eyes in disgust. "He gave me one other option besides sleeping with him—to spy on everyone else in the unit and to report back all their weaknesses. Probably so he could blackmail them for something." Ivy remained silent, sensing he'd tell more when ready. After a few beats, Zain shook his head and said, "For about ten seconds, I thought about spying for him. But then inside my head, I decided to deceive him by saying yes and then report it to the higher-ups the first chance I could."

The fact Zain had resisted the corruption, even when it could've dashed his dream or goal of becoming a Protector, raised him in Ivy's esteem. "Did you manage to report him?"

He nodded. "The next day, in fact. It took a little longer for anything to happen—the officers wanted proof via a recording—but I kept my place, and the other male was reprimanded. However, it made the rest of my time inside the army pure hell. A few humans applauded me standing up to him. But many felt the human had been wronged. I was only a dragon-shifter, after all. And I would flee back to my own clan after a short stint. My word shouldn't have mattered."

Not long ago, Ivy would've agreed with that sentiment.

Now, however, she felt anger at the younger version of Zain who'd done what was right, only to be punished in a different way for it. "Then I sort of understand why you're wary of humans."

He shrugged. "Not all humans. Melanie, Evie, Jane, Emily, and even Rafe have more than earned my respect. Plus, I may grumble, but it's pretty hard to hate someone like Daisy Chadwick."

She smiled. "You're a softie for the hyper, chatty girl, aren't you?"

He grunted, and she smiled wider. Then out of nowhere, an image of Zain holding his own little girl in his arms flashed into her head. He cooed and swayed her, with love in his eyes.

And not only that, but the daughter had ginger hair and blue eyes, just like Ivy.

Panic should have rushed forth at the image, but instead, a slow yearning filled her.

At one time, Ivy had thought of having children. However, her time inside the Knights had quashed that dream. Knights who became pregnant were cast into boring, monotonous jobs inside the organization. To advance—and help rid the world of the dragon infestation—she'd focused only on moving up the ladder and shunned any sort of relationships.

Of course, none of the men who had children were punished the same way. The longer she was away from the Knights, the more she realized the faults. They may have all hated dragon-shifters inside the Knights, but it had clearly favored the men's work over the women's, too.

"Ivy?" Zain queried.

She met his gaze again. "I'm here. I just...I some-times get lost thinking about my past."

"And given how there was angry fire flashing in your eyes, it wasn't about a happy memory, either, was it?"

She should curse Zain's ability to read her so well, but in a way, she liked it. At least for now. "No, it wasn't. But if you can get over what happened to you in the army, then I can focus on the future more instead of the past, and continue to try to make things right."

He leaned forward a fraction, putting their faces about a foot apart. "And just what does this future entail?"

Zain was too close. His heat and scent surrounded her, and combined with the fatherly image she'd conjured up, she wanted to do something ridiculous—lean over and kiss him.

No. Their mating was for convenience, nothing more.

However, she couldn't find it in herself to ignore the dragonman's question. Not after everything he'd shared with her. "I'm still figuring it out. But I'm going to try and be more understanding. I don't know if I can do it all the time, but I want to try to base my feelings, reactions, and responses on the present and what I see instead of what was drummed into me during my time with the Knights."

Zain searched her gaze, his pupils flashing, as he grunted. "From here on out, I'm going to try to do the same when it comes to you."

As they stared into one another's eyes, Ivy's heart rate kicked up, and everything disappeared except for Zain's face.

She was alone with a dragonman, and it didn't bother her at all.

No, instead, it made her want to pull him over and whisper more questions into his ears. Then he'd merely hold her as they talked for hours, exchanging information and learning more about each other.

Could it be possible that this man—no, dragonman—was the one she was supposed to know better than anyone else in the world? Be her partner, and maybe more?

However, Zain cleared his throat, took out his mobile phone as he retreated about a foot, and said, "We should probably go over the questions from my clan members about the data before you get too tired."

And just like that, Zain moved a little further away, and reality rushed back to her.

Unsure of why him moving away should sting, Ivy settled back against her pillows and said, "Then go ahead."

As she answered one question after another, Zain recording them all, Ivy forgot all about her moments of weakness earlier. Maybe with time, she and Zain could be friends. But it was foolish to hope for more.

Chapter Thirteen

As the weeks passed, Zain and Ivy fell into a routine. He'd leave early in the morning to do whatever needed to be done for the Protectors and let her sleep. Around noon, he'd return and eat lunch with her, talking about both the data and the Knights, but also about random things, too.

To be honest, Zain had never talked so much about himself his whole life.

And yet, he now looked forward to his quiet lunches with Ivy. She'd slowly started to do some work with Lucien and Nate in the afternoons, and Zain would help with her physical therapy in the evening.

Ivy would be frail for a while yet, but she had made incredible progress through a combination of dragon's blood injections and physical therapy.

Zain still remembered the first time she'd been able to walk with the use of crutches. Ivy had bitten her lip and moved inch by inch until she'd reached him standing at the other side of the room. Then she looked up at him in triumph, her eyes bright and her cheeks flushed.

He'd nearly lost his self-control in that instant. Never in his life had he wanted so desperately to pull a female close and kiss her.

Yet he'd managed to resist the temptation. Not only was Ivy still weak, the doctors hadn't figured out a complete antidote for her condition.

To kiss or sleep with her could infect him. And neither Sid nor Gregor had any idea how the bloody thing would affect a dragon-shifter.

And that was something Zain needed to remind himself of over and over again. Especially since today was the day Ivy could finally leave the surgery and move into a cottage with him.

His dragon grunted. *It's only a matter of time until Sid and Gregor cure her. Then you won't have a flimsy excuse to hide behind.*

Ignoring his beast, Zain headed down the hall toward Ivy's hospital room. It'd been bloody hard staying away the whole afternoon to allow the doctors time to do their final examinations and tests, but he'd managed it.

In less than an hour, he finally could take his female home and show her a life outside her hospital room.

Zain nearly missed a step and frowned. Ivy wasn't his female, not really. He'd protect her, of course. That was his duty as her mate, nothing more.

His dragon snorted but said nothing.

No doubt his bloody beast was up to something.

He'd just managed to clear his mind of any other

thoughts but taking Ivy home when he knocked on her door and entered.

Ivy sat on the edge of her bed, her feet on the floor, wearing a simple blue dress. It was less formal than the one she'd worn the day of her first trip to the school, but the color made her eyes blaze. When her gaze met his and she smiled, his heart skipped a beat.

It was hard to remember how the female used to be a Dragon Knight. Especially given all the stories Ivy had told him of sneaking out and exploring her neighborhood as a child. She'd had a wild spirit at one time. Maybe it'd come out again soon. Then maybe one day, he could take her up into the air in his dragon form and show her the world from a new perspective.

Of course, he shouldn't be planning so far into the future. After all, Zain hadn't even been allowed to show her his dragon yet.

His beast growled. *Then do it today. If she's well enough to leave the surgery, she's well enough to see us.*

Zain wished he could agree. However, Ivy's constant struggle of progress and setbacks regarding her health had made taking her outside her room difficult. And so anything that could upset her had been banned for a short while. Unfortunately, Sid had included showing Ivy any dragon-shifters in their dragon forms as part of that edict.

Sensing his dragon was about to speak up again, he moved straight for Ivy and smiled down at her. "Ready for the big day?"

She snorted. "I think I can do without staring at a beige, windowless wall ever again. If you tell me the cottage has a room like that, then either you're painting it a different color or I'm never setting foot inside it."

A stray tendril of hair fell over her cheek. Before he could think better of it, he tucked it behind her ear, lingering there a few beats. Her skin was always so soft, and warm, and no female had a scent quite like hers.

Zain was very nearly addicted to it.

And before he could stop himself, he took a quiet, deep inhale. Her female scent was one that haunted his dreams, so sniffing was probably not the best idea. But he couldn't help himself. He answered, "No beige walls anywhere. If anything, it should be the complete opposite of here."

She raised her brows. "Oh, the complete opposite, huh? Well, I'm not sure living in a glass house would be an improvement."

He chuckled. "Of course it's not a glasshouse, bloody woman. You'll just have to wait and see what I mean. After all, you need some motivation to get up and walk all the way to the cottage."

"I suppose," she muttered. "So we'd better get started. It could take me a while."

He reached for her forearm crutches but didn't hand them to her. "As soon as Sid brings the release papers, I will."

Ivy shook her head. "Never in a million years would I have pictured dragon-shifters doing paperwork."

"This is Britain. To not do paperwork to an excessive degree would be a crime."

She raised her brows. "Then violating that crime might be worth going to prison."

Since prison for dragon-shifters was exponentially worse—it was torture to keep their beasts drugged silent and contained for any period of time—Zain changed the subject, not wanting to ruin Ivy's big day. "Are you sure you want to walk the whole way?"

Ivy bobbed her head. "I'm strong enough to do that much, at least. Besides, I don't want the clan to see me in a wheelchair again if I can help it. I'm tired of everyone who doesn't hate me treating me like a delicate porcelain doll."

A female's voice—Nikki's—came from the doorway. "You do sometimes sway on your feet. So it's not like we're being overprotective hens for the sake of it."

Ivy sighed. "Even if you all gang up on me, I'm still going to try walking to my new home."

Zain may be concerned, but a sense of pride washed through him at Ivy's desire to be strong. "Just know that at the first sign of swaying, I'll be carrying you."

"And that's not worse than being in a wheelchair?" Ivy muttered.

However, before anyone could reply, Dr. Sid walked in and stopped next to Ivy's bed. She said without preamble, "You remember your instructions, correct?"

"Yes, yes, check in twice a day via phone and visit the surgery at least twice a week for in-person examinations. And at the first sign of wooziness or anything else that seems off, I'm to call you."

Sid grunted. "Good. I'll be making surprise visits as well, although you've really taken to the healing power of dragon's blood. More than a lot of other humans, which is a good sign."

It was ironic that someone who had dedicated her life to eradicating dragon-shifters recovered faster than most with their blood.

His dragon huffed. *That's not who Ivy is any longer, and you know it.*

Of course I do.

He put out his hand. "Then let me help you up and we can get on our way."

What he didn't say was that there was a surprise waiting for Ivy at their new place. One his nephew and his friend had come up with.

Ever since Daisy's mother had accidentally set off a mate-claim frenzy with Blake Whitby, mated the male, and moved to Stonefire, Daisy was always at Freddie's side.

Trouble was sure to follow. And yet, he hadn't been able to say no to the pair about welcoming Ivy to her new home.

Ivy placed her small hand in his, and he instinctively curled his fingers around hers. She smiled at him, and his heart skipped a few beats again as time stilled.

His mate was beautiful, strong, and clever. And he still couldn't have her.

Not wanting everyone in the room to notice his attraction to the human, he lightly tugged Ivy to her feet, and she balanced with one crutch before releasing his hand and grabbing the other one.

He nearly tucked her hand into the crook of his elbow and ordered her to use him as her other crutch, but resisted. He knew how important it was for his human to make this trip on her own two feet.

Nikki gave him a long look before saying, "Are you sure you don't want me to come along with you two, Ivy? I don't have any duties for a few hours yet."

Ivy shook her head. "I'm fine. Come visit me tomorrow, though, like we planned. Maybe you can finally bring Rafe and Louisa by."

Nikki sighed. "Maybe. If Rafe could put Louisa in a glass container and keep her protected from every little thing in the world, he would."

Ivy smiled. "I still say there must be a dragon-shifter way, way up in his family tree, even if it was only an adopted one."

The shifting gene was always dominant, so it was impossible for Rafe to be part dragon. But merely the fact Ivy could tease Nikki about it confirmed to Zain how much the human had changed since first waking up.

Sid cleared her throat. "As much as I hate to interrupt, it's time to leave, Ivy. This is the least crowded time of the day on Stonefire, and it'll be easier for you to make your way to your new home."

And to avoid unwanted glares was left unsaid.

As Zain had predicted, some people had turned on him and never made eye contact.

But he didn't care. There was so much more to the female than a few years of her past, and one day they'd realize it, too. Especially since she, Nate, and Lucien were getting closer to decoding all the data. That would make the Protectors, and all of Stonefire, that much nearer to destroying one of their enemies.

Zain placed a hand on Ivy's lower back. "Come on.

There's a lot to show you, and I want you to stay awake long enough to check it all out."

She narrowed her eyes. "I can stay awake almost all day now, thank you very much."

"And I can stay awake for several days in a row if need be. So I win."

Ivy muttered, "It's not a matter of winning."

Nikki laughed. "You two really are a mated pair, aren't you?"

Zain felt Ivy still beneath his fingers. Then relaxed and shrugged. "Hatred won't help either of us. Besides, Zain is fun to tease."

Sid motioned toward the door. "Go, or I will find a wheelchair and have Zain forcibly remove you."

While Sid knew about Zain's surprise and was ushering them out for that reason, he didn't want Ivy to think the doctor couldn't stand her. "Work on your bedside manner a bit, Sid."

Sid raised her brows. "I'm doing you a favor here. Now, leave."

Ivy looked between them, but Zain gently pushed her forward. "Fine, fine, we're leaving."

As they walked down the corridor—Zain kept his pace slow to match Ivy's jilted walk with the forearm crutches—Ivy frowned and asked, "What favor was she talking about?"

"It's a surprise. And since you like them, I'm not going to tell you what it is."

She stared at him another few seconds before sighing. "Fine. Then I'm going to walk a little faster."

As she did so, he adjusted his pace. And once they hit

the fresh outside air, Zain couldn't help but glance down at Ivy. The faint sunshine made her hair bright and highlighted the curves of her face.

His dragon spoke up. *You get too much time with her. When will it be my turn?*

Soon enough, dragon. But if we don't get her home and let Freddie and Daisy give Ivy their surprise, we'll never hear the end of it.

His beast snorted. *Look at you, afraid of a pair of children.*

Not afraid, but I'm all for avoiding nuisances. Besides, it'll make Ivy happy.

His dragon fell silent. But Zain barely noticed as he watched Ivy move carefully down the main path toward their cottage, anxious to show her their new home.

Ivy DID her best not to keep looking at Zain despite the fact she could feel his gaze on her face.

Over the last few weeks, she'd grown comfortable around the dragonman to the point she trusted him the most out of anyone on Stonefire.

But it wasn't just trust. Ivy loved how he teased her, and they could talk about anything. Zain had been worse during his childhood than even her. Apparently, when someone could change into a flying dragon, there were so many more ways to get into mischief.

And then there was the fact that any time he touched her or leaned close, she wanted to close the distance between them.

At first, she'd tried to say it was because he'd taken

care of her, spent the most time with her, and even had mated her to protect her.

However, she'd grown close to Nikki, too, and Ivy had no desire to kiss the dragonwoman or rip off her clothes.

Still, Ivy had been able to keep her feelings mostly hidden from everyone but Dr. Rossi. And at least that information was protected because of her patient-client privilege.

The situation would change as of today, though. No longer would she be in a bland, boring hospital room, constantly surrounded by staff. No, she'd be living alone with Zain in their own cottage. Without anyone else around, could she keep herself calm and rational enough to not act on her desires?

Did she need to hide them? It was a lot to ask, but perhaps Zain had shifted his views much like she had.

She was so lost in thought that Ivy barely noticed how Zain turned her one way and then the other until he gently stopped her in front of a small, stone cottage with a few rosebushes and other flowers she couldn't name planted in front of it. He motioned toward it. "Welcome home, Ivy."

Before she could do more than smile, something crashed inside the house, and she jumped.

Zain rubbed her lower back and murmured, "Don't worry. It's part of the surprise waiting inside."

Curiosity piqued, her momentary fear faded. "Then let's hurry up so I can find out what it is."

He helped her make her way up the stairs. When she

reached the top one, a sense of pride surged through her body. "See? I walked the entire way here."

True, she was a little shakier now than when she'd left the surgery, but Ivy didn't care.

Zain said, "You proved me wrong. But it's not the first time, so surely it won't be the last."

He opened the door and motioned for her to enter. Ivy gave him a curious look before heading inside the cottage.

Not two steps inside, Freddie and Daisy rushed toward her and tossed some flower petals. "Welcome home, Ivy!"

Smiling down at the pair, now she understood the source of the crash. "Thank you. I hear there's a surprise for me? Are you two in charge of it?"

Daisy bobbed her head. "Yes, Auntie Ivy. Come on. We need to hurry before Alfie eats it all."

Alfie was Freddie's older brother—Zain's other nephew—and a teenager who could eat the equivalent amount of five people's meals. If Freddie and Daisy's surprise was food-based, she really did need to hurry.

So Ivy followed the children into the kitchen. Daisy motioned toward a lopsided two-tier cake, decorated in white, blue, and green icing. "Ta-da! We made it for you. But we better eat it soon; otherwise it'll fall over. And Alfie says if it falls over, he's going to eat everything that isn't still on the cake stand."

The fifteen-year-old with nearly black hair grinned at Ivy. "We can't let it go to waste. Besides, it'll let me ensure it's not poisoned before everyone else eats it."

Alfie's mum grimaced, as did Daisy's mother. It was

Dawn Chadwick-Whitby—Daisy's mum—who spoke up. "Let's not joke about poison, okay? Now, come on, Daisy-love. Let's divvy up the cake before it falls over and destroys all your hard work."

Ivy felt Zain's presence behind her, but she was focused on his sister, Sasha.

They'd never met. However, she'd allowed Freddie to visit her at the surgery, so she couldn't outright hate her.

Sasha walked over to her and smiled. "It's nice to meet the female who finally turned my brother from a growly grouch into someone who can joke around a little."

Ivy blinked at the compliment. "I didn't do anything."

Zain growled, "Sasha."

His sister ignored Zain and put an arm around Ivy's shoulders. "Come on. You must be tired, and I'll make sure you get the best bits of the cake." She lowered her voice. "Let's just say that the top tier is a bit burnt, so we'll avoid it if we can."

As Sasha chatted about how Freddie and Daisy had spent nearly an entire day on making and decorating the cake, Ivy blinked back tears.

Last year, she'd been hell-bent on destroying dragon-shifters, which included those currently inside her new cottage.

And now, they were welcoming her home with a cake.

Ivy had been wrong, so very wrong, about her early life choices. Which meant she had a lot to make up for.

Because through a pretend marriage, she'd gained a new family of her own. And she wasn't about to allow anything to happen to them, like with what had happened to Richard and David.

So Ivy forced away the tears and did her best to enjoy the moment. Soon enough, she would dig back into the data and her own ideas of how to tackle the drugs of the Dragon Knights.

For the present, she was going to enjoy being welcome and a part of something. And this time, it had nothing to do with hatred. No, it was love and family. And Ivy would die trying to protect it.

Chapter Fourteen

Zain finally shut the front door, meaning he was alone with Ivy in their cottage for the first time.

And rather than go to her, all he did was stand in place and stare at the door.

His dragon grunted. *After all your talk of being strong and being able to resist her, you don't want to risk being alone with her, do you?*

Only because Zain and his dragon had been talking with one another since he was six years old did he dare speak the truth. *A little.*

Don't worry, not even I would try anything with her until she's completely cured. Although letting her know we're interested may not be the worst idea.

He nearly asked who else would be interested? But then he remembered a recent session with Nate, Lucien, and Ivy, and Zain was fairly certain Lucien had flirted with her.

Not that Ivy had said anything or returned the

action. However, that was only the once, when Zain had happened to drop in early one day. Who knew what Lucien said or did when Zain wasn't there.

Maybe he needed to have a chat with the male.

His dragon chuckled. *You want her, so tell her. Otherwise, it's unfair to discourage others. Ivy has been alone for a while, and doubly so with her brother and his partner gone. She deserves some closeness, if she wants it. If you aren't going to give it to her, let someone else do it then.*

When did you get to be so wise and patient?

Ever since you decided to be a bastard in denial.

Zain was about to tell his beast to fuck off when Ivy's voice drifted from the kitchen. "Zain? Are they gone?"

His dragon spoke again. *Go to her. This is a new, unfamiliar place. Make it feel more like a home for her. Our mate shouldn't be anxious if we're around.*

Even a month ago, Zain would've huffed and said that wasn't his job. Being a fake mate meant protecting her but nothing else.

However, his feet had a mind of their own and he went to the kitchen. And the instant he saw Ivy pouring hot water into a teapot, longing crashed over him.

While the simple act of having tea with a female may not seem that momentous to other people, to Zain, it signaled something greater. He could have someone to come home to every day, someone to talk and laugh with, and someone to tease or verbally spar with for fun.

In other words, his life could become so much more than merely his duties as a Protector.

All it would take was him truly accepting Ivy as she

was now, forgiving her past, and making his feelings known.

Could he do it? He could easily face off against a group of dragon hunters with laser weapons, but he hesitated to face a short human female. He'd laugh if it wasn't his own life.

Ivy turned with a smile, although Zain didn't miss the shadows under her eyes. She said, "I don't envy your sister one bit. Those two boys are a handful."

He smiled back at her. Zain went to Ivy's side and helped with the tea. "They were a little easier when they were younger. But being fifteen isn't easy for any dragon-shifter—hormones are surging, your dragon starts thinking about sex, and you have to eat a small mountain of food every day to keep up with both your growth and all of the flight training. As for Freddie, well, it's mostly Daisy's fault. Freddie wasn't as adventurous before meeting her. And now that Daisy lives on Stonefire, I'm waiting to see if the human girl will test even his limits of patience or not."

Ivy tilted her head, a few stray strands of hair falling over her shoulders. Zain itched to wrap the probably silky hair around his fingers but somehow managed to focus on her words instead. She replied, "I think it's good they're so close because it means Daisy will always have an ally. It also helps Daisy adjust to all the changes given Dawn's surprise mate-claim frenzy with Blake and her decision to move to Stonefire permanently."

He shrugged. "Everyone already loves Daisy, so she'll be fine." He searched Ivy's eyes and finally touched a few fingers to her cheek. "I'm more concerned about you."

Zain stroked her cheek a few times, and thanks to his supersensitive hearing, he heard Ivy's breathing speed up to match her thumping heart. When she finally spoke, her voice was slightly husky. "Why are you more concerned about me?"

He leaned closer, reveling in her sweet scent. "Even knowing that you'll have a long road ahead if you stay here, you still want to, right?" She bobbed her head, and he continued, "Then I'll always worry about you, Ivy. Because anyone could turn into an enemy if we're not careful. Even the most rational can turn wild with hatred in extreme circumstances. One attack on Stonefire could trigger that sort of situation. That would put you at risk."

She searched his gaze. "But you're going to protect me, right, Zain?"

"Of course I am. But it may not be enough."

As if in slow-motion, Ivy raised her hand and placed it on his cheek. Both man and beast sucked in a breath at her soft, warm touch. Her voice was like a caress as she said, "I can't think of anyone else I'd want to protect me. I know you won't let me down."

"How are you so certain?" he breathed.

She tilted her head upward, and Zain couldn't resist looking at her full bottom lip. A mouth he couldn't taste or tease because of her condition, although he desperately wanted to. She murmured, "You're my mate. And yes, it started as a duty. But I think it's become more. Or, at least it has to me. What about you, Zain? Am I right about it being more than a duty now?"

As his hearted thundered inside his chest, Zain lost

himself in the blue of Ivy's eyes and debated how to answer her.

IVY DIDN'T KNOW where her boldness had come from, but she was glad she'd touched Zain's cheek and asked her question.

She'd been watching him all day, and while she knew he was softer inside than he let on, the way he played and teased the children had made her belly flip in a good way.

Her attraction had lasted outside her hospital room. And if she was going to live with the dragonman, she needed to be honest with him.

And so she waited for his response, fascinated by his flashing pupils. Not to mention the second his gaze moved to her lips, she couldn't help but lick them.

Rationally, she knew she couldn't kiss him, even if he asked for it because of her unknown condition. And yet, her lips throbbed, wanting to feel his firm ones against hers.

Zain growled. "You know I can't kiss you right now, Ivy, and you're making it bloody hard not to."

She tamped down her joy at his mention of kissing her and replied, "That still didn't answer my question. Am I merely a duty to you, or more, Zain? This is our first night in our new home, and I think we should start off honestly from the get-go."

His pupils finally remained round right before he

spoke again. "The truth will make things difficult, Ivy, and you know it."

Since she'd put everything out there already, Ivy wasn't going to back down. "I don't care. Tell me the truth, Zain. Either do it right here, right now, or I'm going to ask to stay with Nikki or your sister."

He growled, and while she may have flinched in the beginning of their acquaintance, she merely raised an eyebrow in the present. Zain sighed. "The truth?" He moved until he caged her against the counter with his body and arms. The feel of his hard muscles pressed against her body made her knees weak, and not because of her recent awakening from a coma, either.

His hot breath danced against her cheek as he said, "When you first woke up from your coma, I hated you. You represented so much pain for my clan, my friends, and my family. I had planned to interrogate you, find out your secrets, and then allow the DDA to take you away for good."

She searched his eyes as she asked, "So what changed?"

He moved a fraction closer, forcing her to tilt her head further upward to meet his gaze. "I don't know myself what bloody happened, but soon you were more than an enemy. You were interesting, clever, and so very sad. But instead of wallowing, and begging, and another multitude of things you could've done, you were determined to share the encoded data with us. Not to mention you showed patience with my nephew and his friend. And then you looked too bloody beautiful in the blue dress from our mating day."

She blinked. "You noticed my dress?"

One of his arms moved to her upper back. Without thinking, Ivy leaned into the touch, loving the heat of his hand through the material of her top. "Yes, and your hair, and lips, and the deep blue of your eyes. You were supposed to be my enemy, and I resisted for as long as I could. But you're more than the years you spent inside the Dragon Knights, and I want to believe you'll do everything possible to help my clan going forward. Not just for forgiveness, either, but because you think it's the right thing to do."

She swallowed and bobbed her head. "I do. It was easy to hate a nameless mass. But to have something happen to Freddie, or Nikki, or even Bram? It's unbearable. They all risked so much to help me, get to know me, and treat me as a person instead of an enemy." Moving a hand to his chest, she rubbed it back and forth, wishing it was his skin instead of his shirt. "And I didn't say you in that example because whilst I try to be strong, if something happened to you, it'd break me a little inside."

With a growl, Zain hauled her flush against his body and moved his mouth to her ear. "You'd better not be toying with me, Ivy Passmore."

"I'm not," she whispered. "I promise."

Zain nuzzled her cheek with his own, and Ivy melted against him. His husky voice filled her ear again. "My final answer is this. If I could, I would kiss you right now, Ivy, before licking every inch of your body. You started as my duty to protect. But now, you're mine, human. Don't ever think of trying to leave me."

Maybe someone else would be offended at his claim,

but the carefully constructed walls around Ivy's heart tumbled down, allowing the yearning and desire she'd had for her dragonman to rush forth.

Yes, she—someone who had hated dragons to the point she'd given up her life to try to eradicate them— had fallen for a dragon-shifter.

Looping her arms around his neck, she said, "I'm not going anywhere."

"Good." He kissed her cheek for a few beats before flicking her skin with his tongue. She moaned and leaned more against him. Zain growled, "And you'd better believe I'm going to harass Sid and Gregor every chance I get about finding a cure for you."

Emboldened by Zain's words and actions, Ivy kissed his jaw, loving the slight prickle of his late-day stubble. "You won't see me complain."

He laughed, something she'd heard only a handful of times, and it made her heart skip a beat in a good way. He finally replied, "Until then, come sit on my lap, Ivy, and let me make you come with my hand."

She sucked in a breath as the image of Zain's fingers between her thighs flashed into her mind. Wetness surged between her legs. However, the response only reminded her of why she couldn't do it. "No, I don't want to poison you by mistake."

"I have gloves, Ivy. I'm the sort who's always prepared."

She raised her brows. "Prepared to give someone who could possibly poison you an orgasm with your hand?"

"Maybe not for that reason specifically, but now it's all I can think about."

She hesitated. While Ivy wanted Zain more than anything, even the smallest risk of hurting him was too great. "The glove could rip if your talons come out."

"I'll be careful."

"I don't want to risk it, Zain. If you become sick, or worse, because of me, I couldn't live with it. So just share my bed and hold me close. How about that as a start?"

One of his hands moved to the back of her neck and squeezed lightly. "For you, I'll even wear clothes to bed. But just so you know—once you're cured, I always sleep naked. And you will, too."

She laughed. "I think that could be arranged." She traced his jaw, down his neck, and over his shoulder. She continued until she reached the tattoo peeking out from his shirt and traced the design with her fingers. "But the bigger question is how the clan will handle it."

Zain grunted, and Ivy met his gaze again. "You keep helping us to take down the Knights, and they'll have to accept it. If not, they'll have to deal with me and my entire family. Because I think after today, you can see that they are your family too."

She bobbed her head. "I know."

"Good. Now, I'm going to carry you upstairs no matter what you say. I think tonight should be an early night."

Zain moved until he could swoop her into his arms, and Ivy leaned against his upper body, a protest the farthest thing from her mind.

While she should be on cloud nine about Zain feeling the same way about her as she did him, worry niggled at the back of her brain. Because if she couldn't help take down the Knights, it would be more than a little trouble-some. Too many people might think she was deliberately holding back information to protect the Knights.

So first thing the next day, she was determined to find the ad hoc office space inside the cottage that Zain had mentioned was hers and get to work.

Because she had a hell of a lot to lose now if she didn't succeed.

But she couldn't do anything until morning. So she merely enjoyed laying with Zain for an hour or two, teasing him, and eventually falling asleep in his arms.

Chapter Fifteen

It was another few days before Zain could coax Ivy away from her work long enough to show his dragon form. He'd even had to make a bloody appointment to do it.

His dragon snorted. *I'm as anxious as you are, but she's doing important work.*

Something about her on the verge of a breakthrough that would protect all dragon-shifters, not that Zain understood all the scientific jargon. All he knew was that she'd roped in Blake to help her with the math and formulas. If not for Zain's irritation at being separated from Ivy, he might've laughed at how the once hermit-like male had turned extremely growly anytime he was away from his mate.

But at least Blake was mated, which meant Zain didn't have to fight the urge to kill him for giving Ivy the wrong kind of look.

His beast spoke up. *Ivy is ours, and she said as much. And whilst we might not have claimed her yet in bed, we have legally mated her. The clan knows this, so calm down.*

Rich coming from you, dragon. You like nothing more than to flash naked images of her inside our mind.

It helps me with waiting since we only saw her naked the one time.

Ivy had decided that she couldn't be naked around Zain until she was cured. It was too great a temptation.

Never in his life had Zain hated clothing more.

He paced the living room, glancing at the clock. It was five minutes past two. Ivy was late.

Just as he was about to charge into her workspace to see what was going on, Blake emerged into the living room with a smile on his face.

Zain clenched his fingers into a fist and ground his teeth. *Remember, he's not a threat, not a threat, not a threat.*

Blake finally noticed him and blinked. "She's upstairs waiting for you."

Not wanting to encourage the male to go into a long spiel about things he didn't understand, Zain nodded and raced up the stairs to Ivy's office.

He found her hunched over a desk, scribbling furiously. Despite the fact she wore stretchy yoga pants and a loose T-shirt, with her hair hastily tied back, she was still the most beautiful female in the world to him.

While impatient, he merely watched her work. If Ivy was on the cusp of a breakthrough, not even he would be selfish and risk her losing her train of thought.

After all, Ivy was working to safeguard not only Stonefire but dragon-shifters the world over.

When she finally sighed and tossed aside her pen,

Zain took that as his cue to approach her. Without a word, he placed his hands on her shoulders and kneaded the tight muscles. She moaned into his touch and said, "If you ever decide to give up on your Protector duties, you'd be an excellent masseuse."

He snorted. "Right, because my brusque manner will surely put people at ease." He kissed the top of her head and asked, "Did you solve your puzzle?"

Ivy shook her head. "No, but I'm nearly there. There's just one last bit of the formula I need to crack, and I may have something to counter any human-made drug against dragon-shifters. Well, within reason. It won't protect you against something like sarin gas, or other types of biological weapons."

"I think that's fair. Not even you can make us immortal."

She smiled and looked up to meet his gaze. "An immortal dragon-shifter would be far too cocky. I don't think the world would be able to handle it."

He chuckled. "You're probably right." He removed his hands from her shoulders and motioned toward the door. "Can you still come out for a break? My dragon is getting rather impatient for some ear scratches."

She nodded and stood. However, Ivy swayed for a second. Zain steadied her, frowning in the process. "Are you sure you can handle going out? If you're exhausted, then tell me the truth."

"I just need something to eat, and I'll be fine, I promise. And before you get extra protective, Dr. Sid saw me this morning and said I was doing well. She even sent me home with a copy of the results, just in case I needed to prove it to you."

He grunted. "I'm not that bad."

"Oh, yes you are." She placed a hand on his chest. "But I wouldn't have it any other way."

As they stared at one another, Zain battled the ever-present urge to kiss his female. "Since we don't have a lot of time before you need to work some more with Nate and Lucien, I'll take your word. But you're getting an energy bar first."

She sighed. "I hate those things."

"I know, but you need them to gain a little more weight. Doctor's orders." He reached for her forearm crutches and turned them toward the door.

They'd fallen into a routine, and whenever they were inside the cottage, Ivy leaned against him and used him instead of her crutches. However, she wanted to appear less vulnerable outside their home and would only use the crutches then.

The dragon side of him wanted her to always rely on him, but his human half respected his strong, independent female.

After Ivy quickly ate her food, they went outside. As they walked, he noted every person who turned away from them. The list was growing a little smaller as news of Ivy's work spread, but not fast enough.

Every individual who snubbed them was on his list to watch for any sign of danger.

His dragon spoke up. *It takes time. Remember when Melanie first came here? She is merely human, nothing more, and it took months, some even more than a year, to accept her.*

Melanie Hall-MacLeod was beloved not only by Stonefire but also by many dragon clans who supported human-dragon pairings. After all, she'd done much to sway public opinion with her book. *They may have been wary of Melanie, but Ivy's situation is different. There are probably some people who want to kill Ivy for merely being a former Dragon Knight, regardless of what she's doing now.*

His beast growled. *We won't let that happen.*

Agreed.

They approached the main landing area, and Zain mentally sighed in relief to see it empty. He'd picked early afternoon on purpose since it was the quietest time of day for takeoffs and landings.

Ivy whispered, "You're going to keep your promise, right? Not to fly away this first time?"

He placed a hand on her lower back. "No, I won't fly away. And if you want me to change back, you know the special word to say."

She bobbed her head. "Watermelon."

Yes, he and Ivy had a safe word for dragon forms. Zain didn't think anyone had had that before.

He stopped them at the edge of the huge, empty area surrounded by low walls. He turned her face up toward his and searched her eyes. "I know I keep mentioning my dragon's desire to show off to you, but if you're not ready, just tell me now, and we'll do it later."

Ivy shook her head. "No, I'm ready, truly. If I can't accept all of you, then this will be doomed before it barely starts."

He cupped her cheek and stroked her soft skin with

his thumb. "Whilst it may not seem brave to most, you are exceptionally brave right now, Ivy Passmore."

And if not for her condition, he'd kiss her in reassurance.

But he fucking couldn't. Zain was all for getting to know a female he cared for before sleeping with her, but it was starting to get ridiculous.

His dragon murmured, *Forget about that. It's finally my turn to show off.*

Aware of how patient his dragon had been, Zain caressed Ivy's cheek one last time before he moved toward the middle of the sheltered landing area. Methodically, he stripped off his clothes, and he couldn't help but notice Ivy's gaze turn heated. Although the hunger in her eyes made both man and beast stand a little taller, he did his best to tame his cock.

The day he could claim her couldn't come soon enough.

His dragon growled. *Hurry up. You've had a lot of time with her. It's my turn.*

And so Zain closed his eyes and let his dragon half take over so he could shift.

Ivy's MOUTH dropped open as Zain's body changed. His nose elongated into a snout, his arms and legs morphed into limbs, and wings sprouted from his back. It couldn't have been more than thirty seconds or so, but time seemed to move slowly until her dragonman stood in his red dragon form, wings snapped out behind him.

He was tall, so very tall, to the point she had to strain her neck to look upward at his face. The sharp points of his teeth poking out from his mouth made her still a second. But then she met his eyes—eyes that were similar to Zain's when they flashed in his human form—and she let out the breath she'd been holding.

This was her greatest test. And if she failed, it meant no Zain, no closeness, and a life without anyone to call family.

In other words, Ivy would do whatever it took to grow accustomed to his dragon form, no matter if it had once been the stuff of her nightmares.

Zain crouched down as much as he could and folded his wings against his back. When he tilted his head in question, Ivy shook her head to clear the momentary panic and said, "I'm fine, I promise, but just give me a minute to process it all." Taking a deep breath, she added, "Stay there, just like that, okay? So I don't hurt my neck as I look you over."

Zain's dragon form snorted. The humanlike action made her smile. Yes, her man was inside there, too.

The reminder gave her the courage to walk around him, albeit keeping about ten feet between her and the crouching dragon. Even though Ivy had seen a few scales inside a lab, they seemed so much bigger on a dragon itself.

And for a split second, her stomach heaved, thinking of how the Knights had retrieved the scales she'd studied.

Stop it, Ivy. You can't change the past. And yet, as she glanced at some of Zain's talons, she recalled studying those, too.

All of those clinical situations had dismissed the individuals behind those bits and pieces of a dragon.

If only she had a way to convince everyone inside the Dragon Knights of just how wrong their information and fear-mongering was.

Then she remembered that her formulas to safeguard the dragon-shifters were far more important. If the dragons were immune to the Knights' drug concoctions, then they could fight and hopefully defeat the Knights in the near future. Only once the dragon-shifters were safe could she try to help the other humans like herself who'd been persuaded to hate dragons, all because of believing lies.

Ivy made her way around Zain's other side until she stood in front of the dragon's face once more. This time, however, she took a few steps closer and tentatively reached out a hand toward his snout.

When her fingers met the hard, smooth surface of his scales, Ivy stood still for a second, taking in the enormity of the situation. A hand that had once worked so hard to kill the dragons was about to caress one and maybe even scratch behind his ear.

Zain blew a quick breath at her, and she finally met the one eye she could see. It blinked slowly before staring back at her. She knew dragons couldn't talk in their dragon forms, so she sensed it was a form of communication, probably one of reassurance.

She needed to ask Zain more about dragon nonverbal communications later.

But his gesture was the disruption she needed to get out of her head. And so Ivy lightly ran her fingers back and forth against his snout, marveling at the warm yet hard surface of his scales.

Unaware of how long she'd been stroking the same small patch, Zain twitched one ear and then the other. She smiled. "That's right, you mentioned something about how you liked to be scratched behind the ears, didn't you?"

His beast grunted and lowered his head some more. Standing on her tiptoes, Ivy reached behind one ear until she found the tiny stretch of thick skin not protected by scales and then dug her nails in lightly. As she rubbed them back and forth, Zain leaned into the touch and hummed. The sound reverberated down her arm and throughout her body.

Maybe at one time it would've freaked her out or made her scream. But now, the sound and feeling calmed her bit by bit, almost as if the sound reminded her that this was her dragonman. And while she couldn't guarantee every dragon-shifter would do so, Zain would never hurt her.

When Zain lightly bumped his head against her body, she stopped and allowed him to raise his head again. He stood upright a little and motioned with his forelimb for her to stand back once more.

Even though probably ten or fifteen minutes had passed, she nearly pouted as she turned away. She wanted more time with Zain's dragon, to better know the other half of the man she was falling for.

However, Ivy knew Zain was being careful and following Dr. Sid's orders. After all, no one had known how Ivy would react to standing so close to someone who had shifted into their dragon form. Stress, fear, or any negative emotion could trigger her and send her health reeling backward.

So she gave him one last pat and returned to the edges to watch him change back.

The sight of his wings shrinking, his limbs morphing back into human ones, and the dragon face slowly becoming Zain's familiar human one, free of scales and pointy teeth, only solidified that the two halves were truly one.

And no matter what her fears had been or still would be with strangers, she accepted Zain for who he was, dragon and all.

The realization shifted something inside of her a little more. Ivy had been changing her views bit by bit over time, but when it came to her dragonman, she was no longer afraid of any part of him.

If she let herself, she could fall in love with him.

However, Ivy quickly pushed that notion aside. Until she was completely healthy, it was unfair to both her and Zain to think of or wish for such feelings.

So her determination to finish her work to protect the dragon-shifters grew even stronger because now she had more than mere acceptance driving her. She might, just might, even have love in her future, too.

Chapter Sixteen

Every day for the last two weeks, Zain had taken Ivy out and shown her his dragon. Each time the visit was a little longer, to the point he didn't think she had any fear. At least when it concerned him.

His dragon huffed. *Of course not. She is our mate. When she's cured, she'll be begging for us to claim her.*

Some may think his dragon was being cocky, but Zain sensed it was true. They'd been sleeping together, in full pajama-wear, for weeks. He wanted nothing more than to spread his female's thighs and make her scream his name.

But Dr. Sid and Gregor still didn't have a guaranteed cure. Something about a few leads, but they wouldn't risk it yet.

Good thing the doctors had their heads on their shoulders because if it were up to Zain's cock, Ivy would try any and all leads as soon as possible, regardless of the drawbacks.

Pushing the bloody reckless thought aside—his brain agreed 100 percent with the doctors—he replied to his beast, *That will come eventually. For now, Ivy said she wanted to meet us at the surgery. And whilst she said it was nothing bad, I'm uneasy every time she returns there.*

She hasn't gone back into a coma since waking up. She loves us too much to leave us.

Ivy had never said those words to him, but he sensed she might. Zain wasn't the most articulate about his feelings, but the thought of losing Ivy made his heart stop.

And no matter how much he tried to deny it, he was falling for his own mate.

His dragon grunted. *Don't fight it. She will be ours in all ways soon enough.*

As the surgery building came into view, he said quickly, *You can go on about that later. Right now, Ivy needs our help, or possibly our support, with something. So let's focus on that.*

His beast fell silent, and Zain picked up his pace. By now, he was more than familiar with the building's back entrance and had memorized the keypad code required to enter. Dr. Sid's office door was open, but when he peeked inside, only Gregor was there with his and Sid's son—Wyatt—on his lap. Gregor said, "No, Cassidy's not here. They're all in the research lab. But before you go, I wanted to give you a wee update about curing Ivy."

Zain and his dragon went on full alert at the mention. "Did you find something new?"

Gregor bobbed his head. "Aye, we think so. Although there's still some testing left to do. And whilst I wish it was all good news, there's a side effect that you should know about."

"As long as Ivy will be alive and no longer poisonous, I don't care what it is."

Gregor bounced his son and handed the young one a set of toy keys. As the baby gnawed on a bright yellow one, Gregor replied, "You might care about this, though, Zain. What we think is the cure will most likely alter her DNA code a little. And whilst that doesn't seem a big deal, it means that if she's your true mate now, she may not be once she goes through the treatment."

He relaxed a little. Zain had been prepared for far worse. "Is that all? I don't bloody care about her being my true mate or not. Ivy is my female, end of story."

Gregor smiled slowly. "Aye, I thought as much. But I wanted to ask all the same. Your answer proves you care for the lass."

He resisted the urge to verbally lash out at the Scottish dragonman. After all, Zain would owe the male more than anything he possessed if he finally healed Ivy. "Does Ivy know about this yet?"

Gregor shook his head. "No, not yet. Trahern and Emily are doing a few last tests to ensure Ivy's health and safety. And whilst I hate keeping it from the lass, Sid and I thought it best not to distract her from her work. So don't tell her yet, aye?"

"You want me to keep something this important from Ivy?" he asked incredulously.

"Only for a wee while. Sid and I are going to talk to her about it tomorrow. Since it requires using bits of dragon-shifter DNA to make things right, we want to make sure she's okay with that."

Zain's honor was torn. Ivy had been lied to for so

long during her time working with the Dragon Knights, and he'd vowed to always be honest with her.

And now the doctor wanted him to lie. By doing so, Zain wouldn't take Ivy's focus away from her work, work that could protect his entire clan.

For a male who used to believe everything was black and white, it was yet another gray area.

His beast spoke up. *It's more of us not telling her the full truth than lying. And I know that's just as bad, given her past. But let's just check out what she's doing in the research lab first and then decide what to do.*

Zain said to Gregor, "Maybe, but I can't guarantee it. I want to be honest with her."

Gregor nodded. "I'll leave it up to you. If you think she can handle it, then tell her. But if she can't, and her health regresses, we'll have to wait to give her the treatment, and we have no idea what could happen in the meantime. Everyone speaks of you having good judgment, including Sid, so I hope it's true. Either way, just let us know which path you choose."

He grunted, not trusting himself to say something he might regret.

Not wanting to stick around and learn if he had just been put through yet another test, Zain left the office and headed toward the research lab. While he'd never been inside, he'd learned the entire layout of the surgery during his post of watching over Ivy.

So he knocked and waited to see what his mate had to share before he decided what to do about telling her the truth.

Ivy DID her best not to pace. While she didn't always need her forearm crutches anymore unless she was tired, she didn't want to risk tripping and having Zain order a full examination and set of tests to ensure she was fine.

Even though his overprotectiveness could be irritating at times, she smiled. He cared for her, and that made everything else worthwhile.

Although hopefully, after she showed him her work today, he might see her as more than an invalid. True, the doctors still hadn't found a way to cure her condition— poisoning someone with a kiss wasn't something to take lightly—but she believed the day would come.

After all, she'd worked so hard on her recovery, her formulas, and even helping Nate and Lucien with all the data on the thumb drive.

Two of those things might soon make it so that Stonefire could sleep a little easier at night.

Dr. Sid came up to her and placed a hand on her arm. "Maybe you should sit down until Zain gets here."

She sighed. "You of all people should know how much I hate sitting or lying still. Besides, I can stand for hours on my own now, and I'm never taking that for granted again."

Sid looked about ready to argue when a knock sounded on the door. Emily went to answer it, revealing Zain on the other side.

His gaze instantly found hers, and without thinking, she went to him. Zain put his hands on her waist as he asked, "I'm here. So what's going on?"

All she wanted to do was lean against him and revel in his heat and touch, but somehow Ivy stepped back and motioned toward where the three doctors sat around a high table. "Sit down and we'll explain."

She took his hand and guided him toward the table. He sat and tried to place her in his lap, but she shook her head. "Not right now." She murmured, "But definitely later."

Emily sighed happily, but Trahern merely studied the papers in front of him. Ivy knew the other human woman pined for the reclusive dragon doctor and wished she'd remembered that. Ivy didn't like parading what Emily didn't have right in front of her.

Pushing the thought aside, she cleared her throat. There were much bigger things to focus on right now. "Very few people know this information outside of this room, but here goes—I think I finally have a way to protect against any human drugs that can harm you."

Zain blinked. "What? You finally cracked the last part of your formula?"

Ivy nodded. "It uses human blood as one of the ingredients. Dr. Sid came up with something similar not long ago to help a dragonman on Lochguard, but this is for more than countering one specific drug. And whilst we're fairly sure it won't harm any dragon-shifters, the next step is to find volunteers to test it and make sure."

Dragon's blood could heal humans, and it was strange to think that now human blood could help protect the dragons. "Using nonscientific jargon, how is that possible?"

Emily spoke up. "Every drug so far made by the

Knights focused on the differences in our dragon-shifter DNA, but they never attacked or affected humans the same way, probably as a safeguard against their own people. So by incorporating a small bit of human blood —along with some other elements to ensure your bodies don't reject it—it should protect dragon-shifters, too."

Ivy jumped in. "However, the difficult part will be in getting everyone to accept the treatment if the tests go well with the initial volunteers. Sid, Emily, and Trahern tell me that some dragon-shifters view humans like the humans inside the Knights view the dragons—as a lesser type of being, one to be scoffed at."

Zain replied, "It's true, although I don't think that's as much of a problem on Stonefire." He searched Ivy's eyes a second before asking, "But could it really be that simple?"

She shrugged. "I can't say for sure, hence the testing. Kai is secretly reaching out to trusted Protectors and asking them to volunteer for the initial trial. And whilst you're on that list, he said we could ask you in person."

Wily Kai, doing that. Zain would do almost anything Ivy asked of him. Still, he wanted to check with his dragon. *Would you mind?*

No, of course not. Ivy has been receiving shots of our blood for months. Why should I not want to do the same, if it can protect us against the biggest weapon the Dragon Knights have against us?

Zain grunted and spoke aloud once more. "Of course I'll do it, although I hope Kai is doing it in waves, so we're not vulnerable."

Sid answered, "Yes, we are. You and Sebastian are to be the first."

Ivy smiled. "Although you'll be the very first one."

He stood up. "Then let's get it over with."

Sid frowned. "We haven't even gone over the possible side effects yet."

He glanced at each of them in turn. "I trust everyone in this room, not only with my health but to look over Ivy, too. Am I wrong to do so?"

Sid growled. "Of course we'll bloody look over Ivy. I don't like what you imply otherwise."

Ivy placed a hand on Sid's shoulder. "It's okay. He's my mate, and you know how mated dragon males act."

In any other situation, he might've snorted because Ivy sounded more like a dragon-shifter by the day.

Trahern stood, went to the side of the room, and promptly returned with a needle and small vial. "Then let's start. The sooner Zain receives the shot, the sooner we can monitor how well it works."

Emily sighed. "Leave it to you to think only of the data."

Trahern blinked. "What else would I think of?"

Ivy walked over to Zain and touched his jaw. "Are you sure about this? I don't want you to think I'm forcing you, or guilt-tripping you, or some other such thing."

Placing a hand on her waist, he replied, "Don't be ridiculous. You wouldn't do anything to hurt me. Well, in the present. You might've tried to stab me that first day you woke up, if you'd had the chance."

She snorted. "Not likely, since I couldn't manage to hold a knife then. Maybe a few days later, if I'd had the opportunity and resources."

He loved how his female could joke about almost

anything with him. "But truly, it's fine, I want to do this. Besides, if I end up being the first one inoculated against the Knights, then that means I can be on the front lines in taking them down as soon as we have our plan in place."

Ivy caressed his jaw, making both man and beast hum. Soon he could do more than merely touch her skin. He burned to claim her in all ways.

Before anyone could say more, Gregor burst into the room, sans child. He quickly shut the door, glanced at Ivy for a second before zeroing in on his mate. "Cassidy, there's a problem."

Zain stood and faced the Scottish doctor. "What's wrong?"

Gregor glanced at Ivy again before meeting Zain's eyes. "Ivy's picture and whereabouts are all over the human news."

He instinctively pulled Ivy against his side and growled, "Who the bloody hell leaked that?"

Gregor shook his head. "I don't know. But we need to get Ivy to the underground area of the surgery until Bram says otherwise."

Zain was one of the few who knew about the emergency facilities below the building. For Gregor to suggest Ivy had to wait there meant things were a hell of a lot worse than her being mentioned on a news report. "What aren't you telling us?"

Gregor stated, "According to Bram, messages and orders concerning Ivy have already started appearing on the Knights' hidden corners of the internet. It won't be long before they have videos, too, asking for her head. It won't be long before Ivy is going to be target number one."

Ivy leaned against him, and Zain tightened his grip. "Number one target or not, I won't let them take her." He glanced down at his mate. "I won't let them, Ivy. I promise."

He hated the fear in her eyes as well as the fact her voice broke as she said, "I want to be strong, and say it'll all be okay. But it might end up being better to hand me over than risk the entire clan."

He growled. "Don't be ridiculous. You're my mate, which means you're part of Stonefire, too. If you so much as think of running away to sacrifice yourself, I'll hunt you down and tie you to a chair for as long as it takes for sense to return to your head."

Her lips almost smiled. "You would, too."

Sid cleared her throat. "The sooner we get you downstairs, the better. Few know the underground bunker exists, which means you'll be better protected. And whilst I can't guarantee it, it's less likely that whomever leaked the information will be able to give more information about your whereabouts."

Zain growled, "What if it's someone inside the surgery?"

Sid shook her head. "No, everyone who works here has been vetted several times, ever since humans started living on Stonefire. I trust my staff."

Gregor motioned down the hall. "Now, come on. We need to go."

As he and Ivy followed the doctor to a secret entrance, Zain never let go of Ivy. He'd trained nearly his entire adult life to protect the clan, and now he would use those skills to protect his mate.

After all, anyone who dared mess with a dragon-shifter in love was in for a surprise. Both Zain's human and dragon halves would work harder than ever, fighting for the future they'd long wanted but secretly denied.

Whether anyone realized it or not, this moment, right here, right now, was the beginning of the end of the Dragon Knights. Zain would ensure it.

THE NEXT HOUR flew by in a blur as Zain and the doctors secured Ivy in the secret bunker, brought her clothes and anything she'd need to keep working, and set her up for a long stay underground.

She did her best to push down her fears, not wanting to be a burden to anyone. However, when she and Zain were finally alone, she sighed and crumpled down onto the nearby chair. "Whilst I knew the Knights would eventually find out I'm alive and where I'm hiding, it's hard to believe the day is finally here."

Zain crouched down in front of her. He gently lifted her chin until she could meet his eyes. "I wasn't being overly dramatic earlier, Ivy. I will protect you any way I can, starting with me taking that injection you and the others came up with."

She cupped his cheek, needing the familiar heat and light stubble to help steady her. "No, you can't do that right now, Zain. I have no idea if you'll get weak at first, or have a negative reaction."

Zain pupils flashed to slits and back to round. "But without it, I'm too vulnerable. The Knights are bringing war to Stonefire, love. And we're going to have to protect ourselves as best we can."

As she stared into her dragonman's eyes, she wanted to say so much but couldn't. Zain didn't need any distractions, nor did she want to think of this as her last time being alone with him. A hastily said, "I love you," would almost seem as if she were giving up.

And while she had doubts, and probably always would, she had to believe in the dragons of Stonefire. Because if she didn't, then who could she ever believe in?

Zain cupped her cheek, and she leaned into his warm touch. "If you truly want to do it, we should inject you sooner rather than later, just in case there are some side effects. Because if they emerge, it will be within the first few hours, by our best calculations."

He smiled at her, and suddenly Ivy's world seemed a little less dark. No man had ever made her feel that way so easily.

Zain said, "One last thing—did you use your blood for the concoction?"

"No. I'm still poison to others, remember?" Zain looked like he wanted to say something, but Ivy pushed on. "All of the humans on Stonefire donated. This way, no one knows whose DNA is floating inside their veins. We figured that would help with jealous mates."

He smiled wider. "Look at how far you've come, love. Thinking automatically of mates, and their reactions."

She raised an eyebrow. "If that's a surprise to you, about how my views have shifted, then I might have to question your status as the most observant person on Stonefire."

He snorted. "Considering you mated me, and always look forward to scratching my dragon behind the ears, I think it's safe to say I know how far you've come."

Silence fell, and Ivy struggled with what to say. Even though she'd vowed after waking up from her coma not to take life for granted, she had done so to a degree.

Zain was brave and strong and highly skilled, but he could still die. After all, the Knights possessed advanced weaponry to use against dragon-shifters, in addition to their arsenal of drugs. True, the lasers and other anti-dragon guns weren't as reliable, but they could still kill.

She moved her hand from his cheek and reached for Zain's hand. He instantly curled his fingers around hers, the action bringing comfort. She searched his eyes as she said, "Just be careful, okay? I know how much you hate the Knights, but if Kai goes ahead with the plan to take them down once and for all, they will be fighting for their lives. And in that case, they'll try even harder to kill as many dragon-shifters as possible whilst they still can."

Zain brought her fingers to his mouth and kissed the back of them. Despite everything going on, his warm, wet lips against her skin made her sigh with longing.

What she would give to be able to at least kiss the man she loved.

His voice snapped her back to reality. "I've always been careful, but now I have even more reason to do so. You're my heart, Ivy. And they'll have to kill me to keep me from coming back to you."

Her heart skipped a beat—in a good way. "Then

make sure you do. I have a surprise for you, but not until you come back to me after this is over."

"You know how I hate surprises."

She smiled. "I know, but you'll like this one, I promise."

He leaned closer and kissed her cheek, his lips lingering on her skin.

It took everything she had not to turn her head and kiss him properly.

Zain finally pulled back. "I don't want to leave you, but I have to go." She nodded, and he continued, "Stay strong for me, human. Okay?"

She teased, "Well, seeing as I'm going to be doing a lot of sitting whilst down here, forced to take it easy, that should at least make you and your dragon happy, right?"

He chuckled. "A little." Zain sobered. "But it won't be for long if I can help it. I won't let you be trapped in a new kind of prison after being in an unconscious one for so long."

Zain's gruff exterior hid the careful, sensitive man inside. Selfishly, she wanted to hold him and never let him go. However, she knew she couldn't do that, not if she ever wanted a semi-normal life in the future. "I believe in you, Zain. Now, go and come back to me safe and sound."

He kissed her cheek once more before rushing out of the room.

As the door closed, the sound echoed inside the small living area of the bunker.

Not wanting to dwell on her new underground home or how long she had to live there, Ivy powered up her laptop and returned to the decrypted data. Maybe there was something she'd missed, something crucial that could help Zain and the others defeat the Knights.

After all, if her man would risk his life to fight for her, then she wasn't about to sit and wallow about what could happen to her. No, Ivy would fight in her own way, using information and knowledge. She just had to find what she needed first.

Chapter Seventeen

Not for the first time, Zain was glad of his many years working as a Protector because it allowed him to slowly compartmentalize his feelings for Ivy.

He loved his human and had nearly told her so.

However, in the end, he'd decided to tell her after he'd eradicated her greatest enemies.

His dragon sighed. *I don't understand humans at all. We love her. That's it. Why wait?*

Seeing as we're about to go to war, I think you'd adjust your priorities, dragon.

Our mate is just as important.

Not wanting to argue, he ignored his beast as he made his way toward the Protectors' main building.

Even though he'd received his experimental shot to protect against any of the Knights' drugs about an hour ago, he hadn't yet suffered any side effects. The doctors had ensured him it was fast acting and would take hold completely within a few hours.

So now all he had to do was work with Kai to devise a plan for both protecting Stonefire and attacking the Knights' hideouts. Then he could finally join the hunt for taking down one of their enemies. Even a few weeks ago, he would've put the dragon hunters at the top of his list because of what they'd done to his friend Charlie. However, the Knights were slightly ahead in the present.

Zain needed to protect his mate. His late friend would've understood that.

He entered the main security building, nodding to his compatriots as he went. However, Zain managed to avoid any sort of conversation and arrived at Kai's office quickly. With one quick knock, Kai told him to enter, and he did.

Shutting the door, Zain sat in front of his boss's desk, next to Stonefire's clan leader, Bram. Zain said without preamble, "Do you have a plan yet?"

Kai grunted. "No, we're still figuring it out. Much depends on if the protective injections work without killing or not."

Zain gestured toward himself. "I'm alive, aren't I?"

Bram raised his brows and said, "It's only been a few hours. But my stance hasn't changed regarding your mate. We'll protect Ivy no matter what it takes. Don't worry."

His dragon growled. *As if there's any other option.*

Kai prevented Zain from replying to his beast. "Protecting the human is the easy part. Attacking the Knights, and only the Knights, without harming any other humans is our biggest obstacle."

Zain frowned. "The DDA isn't changing their policy, are they?"

Kai shook his head. "No, we've been given permission to fight the Knights on our own and make temporary arrests as long as we alert the DDA as soon as we're done. However, from what Nate and Lucien deduced from the data, most of the Knights' hideouts are in populated areas. That's a massive problem."

Bram said, "There are two ways to handle this, but Zain won't like one of them since it involves Ivy."

Trying his best not to lash out at his clan leader, Zain forced his voice to remain even as he asked, "What's the option that doesn't include Ivy?"

Bram shrugged. "Asking the British Army for help. Rafe says he can probably make it happen, if we ask nicely."

Rafe Hartley was not only a former soldier but also the human mated to Nikki. He currently served as the army liaison between the humans and Stonefire. While Zain trusted the officers less than others because of his past, he might not have any other choice but to rely on them. After all, he wouldn't let anyone use Ivy as bait.

He looked between Bram and Kai as he said, "So tell me what the army plan involves."

Bram raised an eyebrow. "I didn't think you'd jump on working with them so quickly."

Damn his clan leader knowing too much. However, Zain didn't alter his neutral expression one bit as he said, "If given the choice between putting your mate in danger or asking humans you may not completely trust to help you, which would you choose?"

"Fair point," Bram stated. "Well, here's what we have come up with so far."

As Bram explained the plan, Zain thought it might work. Especially if he and the handful of other inoculated Protectors could work alongside the humans in the army.

Zain hated putting everyone's life on the shoulders of the British Army, but he didn't really have a choice. He only hoped that relations between the human and dragon-shifter soldiers had improved over the last decade. Because otherwise, they would have to think of a different plan, one that probably involved using Ivy as bait. And once his mate learned of how she could help, she'd bloody volunteer.

And there was no fucking way Zain would allow that to happen.

Ivy FINISHED the last bite of her sandwich and pushed away the empty plate, engrossed with the information on the screen in front of her.

Could it be true? Had she finally found something that could help Zain and the others take down the Knights?

Wanting to be doubly sure, she reread the passage in question:

As more and more of the dragons fully recover from our chemical attacks, retreat and destroy plans need to be solidified so we can fight another day. The hardest part will be putting everything in place as quickly as possible, as the need to implement a network-wide plan increases by the day.

The most likely scenario to reach everyone will be to broadcast a phrase to all members at the same time, blasted through every form of communication possible, both in-house and through leaks to human news agencies. While concrete plans need to be made and approved, a reference to the true founder of the Dragon Knights, and mention of his sacrifice fighting off the dragons, is probably the best method. Every member learns early of the name and the sacrifice. And as far as we know, no dragon or human dragon ally will understand what it means.

Leaning back, Ivy let out the breath she'd been holding. No, most wouldn't know the information as it was a closely held secret, one only revealed to those who had completed all lessons and therapy sessions with the Friends of the Worlds, right before they were inducted to the Dragon Knights. The strict measures and involved steps ensured that outsiders didn't know the truth of how the Knights were founded.

But Ivy knew all of that, and more.

And it was easy to see how the others going through the information from the thumb drive would've dismissed the passage she'd just read. After all, outsiders would have no idea what the vague statements referenced.

Which meant that if Ivy leaked the information about the founder to the media and had Lucien and Nate blast it online through discreet channels, it might just trigger the Knights to scurry and try to flee. And if the dragon-shifters and DDA were waiting for them, they could be captured with minimal loss of life.

However, the plan wouldn't be completely free of

death since some of the most devoted Knights would go down fighting until they took their last breath. Still, it was better than Stonefire and their allies going in blind and trying to fight their way to a victory.

And her gut said it would work.

So Ivy quickly opened a black document on her laptop and typed up everything Stonefire and the others would need to know to implement her idea. Sure, she planned to phone Sid and the others as soon as possible. But just in case she passed out again before she could share the information—there was always a chance it could happen until she was fully cured—her sending it now would ensure they had it.

As she typed like lives depended on it—which they did—the screen began to swim before her eyes. Shaking her head, she pushed on until she clicked the Send button in her email.

That done, she put her head in her hands and closed her eyes. The pounding in her head was akin to someone hammering her skull, and despite the fact she'd just eaten and had spent the last few hours sitting on a couch, she was lightheaded.

Something was wrong.

Ivy reached for the emergency alert button near the sofa to call either one of the doctors or trusted nurses looking after her. However, before she could reach it, the world went dark.

Chapter Eighteen

*Z*ain sat with Kai, Bram, and Nikki, discussing the email Ivy had sent several of them—a brilliant bit of information that had shifted their plans—when someone knocked on the door and entered.

Jane looked around the room, her expression grim. Kai was the first to ask, "What's wrong, Janey?"

"It's Ivy—she's unconscious."

Standing, Zain barked, "Tell me everything, now."

Jane didn't even raise an eyebrow or scold him, which told him volumes. She replied, "There's not much to tell. Dr. Sid and Gregor are trying to figure out what happened. All I know is that one of the nurses found her unconscious on the floor and barely breathing."

He rushed up to Jane. "Where is Ivy now?"

"Somewhere in the surgery, but Dr. Sid is keeping her location a secret for now."

Ignoring his pounding heart—Zain wouldn't let fear

overtake him—he turned to Kai. "I have to go check on her."

"Go. We have this covered."

Not waiting for another word, he raced out of Kai's office, down the corridors, and out of the building.

Even though the doctors had always said Ivy could relapse at any point until she was fully cured, his gut said something else was at work here. Because the blast of Ivy's location and being alive on the news earlier in the day, forcing her into hiding, seemed too much of a coincidence.

After all, it would only take one person with the knowledge of her location and a hatred of the Dragon Knights to try and harm his human. Handing her over to the Knights wouldn't be enough for more than a few dragons harboring a grudge.

His dragon spoke up. *If someone reached her, we'll find out who and take care of them.*

No killing, though. You know better than that.

His beast growled. *It's our mate, the female we love. We should rightfully be able to get retribution.*

Let's see how she is and what the doctors know before planning a revenge operation.

You're too fucking calm.

One of us has to be right now, if we want to help Ivy the best we can.

His dragon paced inside his mind but at least remained silent as Zain entered the back entrance to the surgery building.

Emily Davies emerged from one of the rooms he

passed and called after him. Zain turned around and barked, "Where is she?"

The human was used to dragon-shifters and their orders after living on Stonefire for so long, so didn't bat an eyelash. "Come with me. And save your questions for later, or I'll put you in a waiting room until Dr. Sid or Gregor has time to speak with you."

Even though Zain could probably punch a hole into the wall of any room in the building and find a way to escape, he merely grunted. "Fine."

The female guided him toward one of the smaller storage rooms. Only once the door was closed did she move toward the back and pushed against a section of the wall. It clicked and slid open, revealing yet another secret entrance, but one he hadn't known existed.

Since all he cared about was finding out what had happened to his mate, Zain didn't ask anything about it lest Dr. Davies carried out her threat to leave him somewhere to wait in agony.

After descending several flights of stairs, the human finally stopped at a door, pressed her thumb to a small scanner, and entered the area.

He barely paid attention to the number of doors or the layout. His mind kept trying to play out the worst-case scenarios for Ivy, and it took all of his energy to push them back.

Right now, his mate needed him to be strong for her. He couldn't suffer any distractions.

Emily finally stopped in front of a door at the very end of the hallway and stated, "Promise me that you won't start yelling at the doctors, and we'll go in, but not before."

In any other situation, he would've admired the human's strength. However, Zain merely replied, "Yes, fine, I promise. Now, show me Ivy."

She opened the door and moved out of the way. What he saw made him stop breathing.

Ivy lay pale—paler than usual—in a hospital bed, hooked up to a ventilator and various monitoring devices. And even though he'd watched over her for nearly a year when she was unconscious, she'd at least breathed on her own during that time.

Her condition was worse, much worse, this time around. She might die.

He rushed toward her, but Gregor stepped in front of him. "Not yet, lad. We need to talk to you first."

Clenching his fingers into a fist, Zain gritted out, "About what?"

Gregor's voice was softer as he said, "I know you want to touch your mate, probably talk to her, and try to comfort her. However, she's in critical condition right now. And even the slightest movement could send her over the edge."

Never taking his eyes off Ivy's face, he asked, "What's wrong with her?"

Gregor didn't miss a beat. "She's been poisoned. Not the same as the one used on her with the Knights. Nor would the dosage we think was used on her normally be enough to put someone into such a critical condition. However, with her underlying one, it was enough."

Despite the fact man and beast wanted to rush over

and hold their mate close, and tell her to hold on, Zain forced his brain to work. "So someone knew what they were doing."

Emily chimed in. "It seems so. If Nurse Ginny hadn't found her when she did, it might've been too late."

His beast roared at the possibility. Zain managed to remain the calmer of the two of them. "Can you help her?"

Emily was the one to reply. "We think so. If we use the treatment Sid and Gregor talked to you about, it may be enough to move her from critical to merely feeling ill for a few days."

He snarled, "Then why haven't you fucking done it already?"

Unfazed, Emily stated, "We need your permission since we can't obtain it from Ivy herself."

"Do it, and quickly."

Gregor stepped in front of Zain, blocking his view of Ivy. Zain was about to tell him to move when the doctor said, "I can't guarantee it will work, Zain. You need to understand that. It could make things worse since the treatment didn't factor in her recently weakened state."

"Is there any other way?" he demanded. When both doctors said no, then Zain motioned toward Ivy. "She'll die without any treatment, right?"

Gregor nodded. "Correct."

"Then fucking give her the treatment."

Emily said softly, "You may want to wait outside, then. We can't risk your dragon taking control and stopping us partway through the process."

His dragon snarled, *I would never do anything to endanger our mate. Tell them so.*

Are you sure? I don't want to leave Ivy, either. But if she's in pain, you may lose reason.

I won't bloody lose my head. We should be here.

Just in case she doesn't survive was left unsaid.

Pushing aside the negative thought—Ivy needed as much hope and positivity as he could muster—he looked at each doctor in turn. "We'll both behave and stay out of the way. Just help her, please."

Gregor studied his eyes a second before nodding. "Aye, then let's get to it, Emily." He motioned toward the side of the room. "Wait over there until we say it's safe to approach your mate, Zain."

Zain followed the order and stood out of the way. He watched as the pair took something from a refrigerator, prepped some medical supplies, and then stood to either side of Ivy as they laid a large, blanket-like object over her.

It was difficult to see her with the tube in her mouth and wires attached to various parts of her body. His female had come so bloody far, fought with all her might to merely walk again, and was back at point zero.

His beast murmured, *She will walk again. There's no way she'd let us carry her everywhere.*

He almost smiled. *No, she wouldn't, would she?*

Gregor finally met his gaze again. "We're going to start. The first part will be the most difficult as we need to lower her body temperature before we administer the treatment. Are you ready?"

As soon as he bobbed his head, Gregor and Emily

murmured some last instructions to one another before Emily flipped a switch.

At first, it seemed like nothing happened. But soon, the machine used to monitor Ivy's vital signs beeped faster and faster. While he wasn't a nurse or doctor, he knew what most of the displayed information meant.

Ivy's body temperature was dropping. Fast.

Every muscle in his body itched to dash over, tear the blanket-like object off her, and hold her close to warm her up.

But he trusted the doctors. Even if he sometimes complained about the Scottish bloke, Sid would never have put up with, let alone mated, an idiot.

As one second passed, and then another and another, Zain clenched his fingers into fists and resisted rushing to his mate's side. The treatment wasn't something he could do, and it killed him that he couldn't protect his mate in all ways.

His dragon said, *No one can. Even I know that.*

Emily quickly flipped the blanket down, and Gregor administered one, two, three different injections before Emily put the blanket back. Both watched the monitors, waiting for something, although he had no idea what.

As the machine beeped louder, Zain couldn't contain his growl. For all he knew, she could be dying. "Help her," he ordered.

Emily never removed her gaze from the monitors. "Nearly there."

Two seconds later, she flipped a switch, and Gregor administered one last injection.

That's when Ivy's body temperature began to rise.

Each degree it climbed, his heart slowed down a fraction. He had no fucking idea if she was out of the woods, but at least she wouldn't die of hypothermia, or whatever it was that could kill someone with a low body temperature.

After what seemed like hours—but was probably only minutes—Gregor finally turned toward Zain. "Come stand by her side and talk to her. She needs to hear your voice."

Not needing a nudge, he rushed over but didn't touch her yet. "Does this mean she'll recover?"

"We won't know until she wakes up or starts breathing on her own. But if you're extremely gentle, you can hold her hand to let her know you're here."

Emily placed a stool near the bed, Zain sat, and gingerly took Ivy's hand in his.

Her skin was like ice, and her fingers completely lax.

So different from when she was awake and tugging him toward her latest breakthrough or attempt at cooking.

He'd suffer a million burnt soups and sandwiches to merely see her smile again.

Zain cleared his throat to help push back the emotions that threatened to spill forward. He wanted to tell Ivy how much he loved her, needed her, couldn't live without her. Only then would he scold her for nearly dying and threaten to bring her back to life only to kill her again if she left him.

However, he'd never been a male who easily expressed feelings in front of others. So he gently squeezed her hand and murmured, "Come back to me, love."

Gregor placed a hand on his shoulder. "We'll give you a few minutes alone, aye? However, press the call button right there next to the bed at the slightest change in her condition."

He nodded. "I will."

"Good. Either Emily or I will be back soon to check on you both."

Zain barely noticed as the doctors finished cleaning up and left him alone with Ivy.

As soon as the door closed, he whispered, "Ivy, love, wake up so I can tell you how brilliant you are. That plan of yours, the one to take down the Dragon Knights, is something we never could've done on our own. And if everyone on Stonefire doesn't realize how clever you are, or that you're devoted to protecting us, then I say chuck them out of the clan as soon as possible."

Ivy remained motionless.

Zain's entire world verged on one experimental treatment. And as he stared at his mate's pale face, all thoughts of taking down the Dragon Knights faded to the background. His female was his future, no matter what happened to the Knights. And she needed him now more than ever.

So he settled down, told her one childhood story after the other, hoping that at some point she'd open her eyes and tell him to stop talking.

Chapter Nineteen

Noises filtered into Ivy's strange dream of riding on the back of a dragon, the tall buildings of London speeding below her, along with the River Thames.

And yet as she went along, chatter came from behind her—the sound of children. She wasn't alone on the dragon's back, which made her frown. If she could barely hold on, then children should most definitely not be on a flying dragon.

She shouted as much to the dragon, but the beast kept alternately beating its wings and gliding on the air currents.

Ivy needed to at least make sure the children quieted down and held tightly onto her. However, as she tried to turn around, she couldn't move, no matter how hard she tried.

Then the noises grew louder until one finally became audible, "Come on, Freddie. We should go again. You might win finally."

The reply faded into a garble Ivy couldn't understand.

Why would Freddie and Daisy be in her dreams? Not to mention what sort of game could they play on the back of a flying dragon?

Then the dream-dragon instantly appeared along the White Cliffs of Dover. A beat later, it dove straight for the English Channel, and she screamed as the beast pulled up at the last second, skimming the water with its talons.

Daisy's voice filtered through once more. "Auntie Ivy? Are you okay?"

Then Zain's voice filled her ears. "Ivy, love, are you there? Can you open your eyes?"

Zain. She yearned to feel his arms around her, his heat and scent invading her senses.

But Ivy couldn't make her eyes work, let along move anything else.

Had she fallen into another bloody coma?

Someone touched her face. "Ivy." It was Zain again. "Come back to us, love. Please."

The gentle, begging tone of his voice didn't sit right with her. Zain was supposed to be strong and stubborn, and most definitely not pleading with her about something.

Maybe she was dying.

Rather than let the thought terrorize her, it only strengthened her resolve to open her eyes.

Concentrating, she imagined light invading her pupils, allowing her to see everyone and everything in the room.

After who knew how much time passed by, she

managed to crack her eyes. And then a bit more, until light temporarily blinded her.

She blinked a few seconds before she clearly saw Zain, Daisy, and Freddie, all standing around her bed, looking down at her.

Zain was the first to speak. "There you are, my human. It's about bloody time you woke up."

She wanted to growl but barely managed a croak.

Smiling, Zain leaned down and whispered, "You can scold me soon enough, love." He gently kissed her cheek, the warmth of his lips on her skin giving her a rush of strength. "But for now, just try to keep your eyes open until the doctors arrive."

Daisy raised her hand. "I'll go get them!"

Zain said to her, "Take Freddie with you."

The pair raced out of the room, leaving her alone with Zain.

As she looked into his deep brown eyes, she struggled not to cry. She had no idea why she'd been out again, but now that she was awake, she was grateful she could be with her mate again. Maybe it was selfish, but she didn't want him to move on and be with anyone else since she'd barely had any time alone with him herself.

She hadn't even told him how she loved him yet.

After that, she'd be a little more magnanimous.

He stroked the hair away from her face as he said, "I'm here. I'll always be here."

Maybe some would think it was hyperbole, but she knew he'd been by her side as much as possible.

They continued staring into one another's eyes—Ivy trying to convey how much she wanted him to hold her and never let go—until a few people rushed into the room. Dr. Sid's brown eyes and pony-tailed head came into view first. "Move, Zain. I need to examine Ivy."

She expected Zain to growl, but he merely complied, moving so Dr. Sid and Emily could both be at her side.

Ivy wasn't sure if she should be worried about his complacency or not.

Dr. Sid spoke first, as she flashed a small light into Ivy's eyes. "Can you talk yet?"

It took a lot of effort for her to say, "No."

Sid smiled. "That was a word." Her face returned to its normal stern expression. "Since you're probably curious about what happened to you, I'll explain it all as Emily checks you over." As Sid recounted how someone had poisoned her, as well as the doctors trying the experimental cure, Ivy's jaw would've dropped open if she could've managed it.

Dr. Sid added, "However, the fact you're awake is a good sign, a very good sign. You might be past the worst of it yet."

With a bit of effort, she croaked, "How long… to…recover?"

"I'm not sure. But the good news is that your most recent blood tests show you're no longer poisonous to anyone. So once you're strong enough, you can finally kiss your mate." Sid looked at Zain and raised her brows. "Don't think of trying it earlier than when we say you can do it, either."

Something passed between Sid and Zain, some kind of information they didn't want to tell her.

And as much as she wanted to demand answers, her

throat ached and her entire body was heavy, sort of like when she'd first woken up from her coma.

If—no, when—she could walk on her own two feet again, she'd never take it for granted.

Emily finished her quick examination, nodded, and met Ivy's gaze. "Everything seems normal right now. I need to draw more blood, but then you can have some ice chips and spend a bit of time alone with Zain."

Zain snorted. "We'll see if that comes true or not. Daisy has tried to be in this room as much as possible, something about having a lot of energy and wanting to give Ivy some of it to help her wake up and walk again."

She attempted to laugh, but it turned into a quick, dry cough.

Emily nodded to herself. "Right, then let me draw your blood so Zain can help you with your throat."

As the doctor quickly did so, Ivy couldn't tear her gaze away from Zain. To most people, he'd look nonchalant and in control.

But she'd spent a lot of time with her mate—at least when she'd been conscious—and she noticed the faint circles under his eyes and the overly long stubble on his cheeks.

She hated that she'd been the one to cause him distress. But once she was well, she would make it up to him.

Starting with their first bloody kiss on the lips.

ZAIN DID his best to remain calm as he watched the two

female doctors do their work. But on the inside, he was a wreck.

He wasn't a male who cried often, but when Ivy had finally opened her eyes, he'd nearly done it. Only the two children in the room had prevented him from breaking down.

The doctors had said that once Ivy woke up, the worst of the danger should be over.

"Should" being the operative word, but he'd take it.

And now his mate was awake, staring at him from across the room, her beautiful eyes conveying more than anything she could say in the moment.

He couldn't wait to talk with her without anyone else listening.

His dragon spoke up. *You'd better bloody tell her you love her when you get the chance. No more waiting.*

I agree, no more waiting, dragon.

Good. And once you do that, then hold her, kiss her jaw, her cheek, her temple, and say it again.

Zain mentally grunted. *Someone's becoming romantic.*

Don't tease me. You know how close she came to dying. If you won't treasure her, then I'll take control and do it myself.

Zain mentally growled. *Of course I'll treasure her. Just let the doctors do their work first, okay?*

Fine.

He went back to watching the doctors work on Ivy, the time ticking by slowly.

When Emily finally finished collecting her blood sample, she left the room. Dr. Sid finished whispering something into Ivy's ear before walking over to him. The doctor said, "I can give you five minutes with her, but I really want a nurse or doctor in here with Ivy for the first few hours to monitor things closely."

Just in case Ivy experienced any of the side effects the doctors had disclosed.

One of which meant she could fall back into a coma —one she'd never wake up from.

His dragon chimed in. *She just has to make it through one day. If Ivy survives the first twenty-four hours after waking up, the doctors are fairly confident she'll make a full recovery.*

Only twenty-three hours and forty-two minutes to go.

Zain finally replied to Sid, "I'll take whatever time with her I can get." He lowered his voice to a level only a dragon-shifter would be able to hear. "And before you ask, no, I'm not going to leave and find sleep somewhere else. Not until Ivy passes out of the danger zone will I do more than go into the attached toilet."

Sid bobbed her head. "I completely understand." She laid a hand on his bicep. "We're one step closer to this being over, Zain. Then you can finally enjoy having a mate."

With that, the doctor left, leaving him alone with Ivy.

He met his mate's eyes again and walked slowly toward her until he stood next to her bed. Never breaking his gaze, he took her hand in his and said, "I love you, Ivy."

She smiled faintly. Then her scratchy voice whispered, "I love you, too."

Even though he'd suspected as much, the words sent a rush of euphoria throughout his body, making his heart warm. "I'm sure some people would've waited until you were fully recovered, but I couldn't, Ivy. I put it off too long before you were poisoned, and I wasn't going to let the chance pass by again."

"Well, a little passed."

He snorted and then lightly caressed her cheek with a finger as he replied, "I'm glad your humor is still intact." Leaning down, he kissed her cheek and murmured, "Soon enough I'll be able to kiss you properly, and teasing me should be the last thing on your mind."

"Don't tease me."

At the scratchiness of her voice, he remembered her throat. Kissing her cheek one more time, he reached for the cup of ice chips and sat on the side of her bed. He placed a small piece of ice at her lips—lips that were full and tempting despite how he shouldn't notice, showing his selfish side at wanting to kiss her right then—and slowly fed her one, and then another. After she finished with the second one, he finally spoke again. "I'll always tease you, love. So if you can't handle it, then maybe you should petition for a divorce right now."

She rolled her eyes. When she replied, her voice was less scratchy. "Just before I can finally kiss you, you want a divorce."

His dragon growled. *Don't let her think that.*

She's joking.

I don't care. Treasure her, remember.

I will, but I won't smother her with overprotectiveness so soon, either. She'd hate that.

Ivy's voice interrupted his conversation. "What does your dragon have to say?"

"He's being more overprotective than you've seen before."

His mate smiled faintly. "Just tell him that I'll give him loads of ear scratches as soon as I can manage it. Maybe that will help calm him down."

It's a start. But until we fully claim her, I won't be calm. At all.

Ignoring his dragon, Zain said to Ivy, "He'll like it, of course." He gave her another ice chip before adding, "But being able to kiss you will help even more."

Once she finished the ice, she asked, "Who will it help more—you or the dragon?"

"Both," he stated without missing a beat.

"Me too." She reached out to touch his thigh. Despite the thick material of his jeans, it burned his skin. She continued, "But it's still going to be a while, right? In case it kicks off a mate-claim frenzy?"

Zain decided to be honest with her. "Even if you were mine before—and I don't know for sure if that was true—it may not happen now, Ivy. The doctors didn't have time to explain it to you, but the treatment they gave you alters your DNA a fraction, enough to make you appear a different person to a dragon's instinct."

Maybe if she hadn't met Zain or formed friendships during her time on Stonefire, she might've reeled from the news. However, being alive—especially given her chance at a future with happiness—was more important than subtly altered DNA.

She finally replied, "Either way, it doesn't matter to me." She hesitated before asking, "Will you be disappointed if I'm not?"

He growled before cupping her cheek. "Of course I

bloody won't be. You're mine, human. So get used to that idea."

"I think I just might be able to, as long as I get to say you're mine, too."

Zain wanted to kiss her until they were both breathless, but somehow, he managed to only stroke the soft skin of her cheek with his thumb. "Everyone already knows I'm yours, but you can make signs and post them on the cottage front door if you like, just to be sure."

She laughed, and even if it was a bit scratchy, it was music to his ears. He loved each and every time his mate laughed, and he would work harder to make it happen more often.

His dragon snorted, clearly in a better mood now. *No one will believe you could do that, even if they see it.*

We've seen over and over again how a good mate can change a dragon-shifter for the better. Why would people not believe we can make ours laugh?

His dragon sighed. *Because some will never believe a dragon and a former Knight could truly be happy.*

Well, fuck them and their ignorance. Because I'm not giving up our human.

Zain finally spoke aloud again. "Be prepared to be spoiled for a while, and not just by me, either." He gestured to the drawings on the wall. "Daisy has become quite taken with you, and has spent most of her time here with Freddie, drawing furiously to decorate your room."

Ivy's gaze darted around to the different walls before meeting his again. "I love them. It's much better than before, when no one wanted anything to do with me. At least now I have two children who want to be friends with me."

Not wanting Ivy to remember the tumultuous first weeks after waking up from her year-long coma, he focused on Daisy again. "Don't worry, you'll have more than enough drawings to use at home, too. Daisy has persuaded Tristan and other teachers to have their students make pictures for you as well, ones depicting different aspects of dragon-shifter history."

She smiled again finally, and the sight made him relax a fraction. "Normally I don't like to rely on others' versions of history, but I think I'll make an exception this time."

He snorted. "If you can even figure out what they are about. Some of the young ones' art is one massive collection of colors."

"That doesn't matter. I'll still treasure them."

As she fell silent, he wondered if she thought about their own children one day.

Pushing the thought aside—his first priority was Ivy above all else—he changed the subject. "On behalf of all of Stonefire, thanks for the email and idea you sent us about how to take down the Dragon Knights."

Ivy perked up a little. "Will Kai and the others use it?"

"Probably, although with a few additions of his own. He and the DDA are in the midst of talks right now."

Ivy opened her mouth to probably ask more questions, but someone knocked on the door before Sid walked in.

And while Zain knew Sid only wanted to help, a

small part of him wanted the doctor to go away for a bit longer.

His dragon spoke up. *Now who's impatient?*

Shut it, dragon.

As Zain watched Sid ask Ivy questions and reveal her preliminary blood results—which were promising—the image of him standing next to Ivy in the surgery, her holding their child, flashed back into his head.

Yes, he wanted that future. Which made him accept something that had been floating around the back of his mind—he'd have to give up his chance to take down the Dragon Knights. Supporting Ivy, loving her, and ensuring she knew she needed to stay alive was far more important than one mission or operation.

And given how Kai and the DDA wanted to act sooner rather than later, Ivy would still need him when everything went down with the Knights. However, he would continue helping Bram and Kai deal with the traitor who'd given up Ivy's location. That would have to be enough to appease his beast when it came to protecting their female.

Chapter Twenty

Two weeks later, Ivy sat upright in her bed inside the hospital with Zain at her side and wished for once her mate wasn't there.

The dragon clans of the UK and Ireland, as well as the Department of Dragon Affairs in both countries, were about to start their mission to take down the Dragon Knights once and for all.

Not able to stop herself, she said, "You should be with them, Zain."

He sighed as he cuddled her closer against his side. "We've been through this a million times, love. You need me more."

She bit her lip to keep from rehashing her reasoning.

Ivy had survived the first twenty-four hours after receiving her special treatment and had been doing better each day.

Dr. Sid said it was only a matter of days before she could go home to her cottage with Zain.

In other words, she was on the mend and didn't need constant supervision.

Her mate hadn't agreed, of course, despite his experimental treatment also succeeding and thus protecting him against any of the drugs the Knights may have. Instead, Zain had only encouraged others to volunteer for the shots, too.

Not that any of her arguments for him going mattered anymore. It was past the point of no return—the operation would start in a matter of minutes—so she snuggled against him and played with the small peek of chest hair at the neckline of his top.

Both of them stared at the speakers on the side table, ones that would broadcast the most important information to certain individuals inside Stonefire.

Zain had fought with Kai and Bram about it, saying Ivy needed to hear it all, too, for closure.

And while she'd tried to give half-hearted protests, she secretly agreed she needed to hear everything play out in real time.

Maybe if she was on her own, hated by everyone around her, it might've been too much to take in.

However, as she breathed in Zain's scent and soaked up his body heat, she wasn't alone.

She never would be again.

The thought erased some of her tension, and Ivy finally spoke again, gesturing toward the speakers. "Thank you again for arranging it all."

He smiled down at her and kissed her forehead—doctor's orders still didn't allow them to kiss on the lips yet. "We'll see how Dacian does as an announcer."

The young dragonman had passed all his final tests with the Protectors and was a full-fledged one now. However, he was still new, and the newest member had been stuck with the announcer task. "Well, he likes football a lot, so hopefully all those years of watching matches will give him an idea of how to make it interesting."

Zain snorted. "He'll be receiving information from multiple sites simultaneously, with only Nate, Lucien, and Hudson to help him. He'll probably be overwhelmed to the point where making it entertaining will be the least of his worries."

She shook her head. "It's not entirely true that he'll be doing it with a team of three. The other dragon clans in the UK and Ireland each have people helping to sort all the information, too."

He grunted. "Maybe. Technology will help him, for sure. Something like this would've been a hell of a lot more difficult even thirty years ago."

Dacian's voice came over the speaker, preventing them from saying anything else. "The Knights have received their coded warning thanks to the IT specialists' plant and have begun their mass exodus. Everyone is in place to capture them as they flee."

Ivy stopped breathing a second, desperately wanting to hear what happened next. For all she knew, there could be new escape routes or procedures, ones that could ruin the whole thing.

Everyone would truly hate her then and think she misled them all on purpose.

After a few seconds, Dacian spoke again. "It's

confirmed—every major Knight hideout and operation center has been discreetly surrounded, and the most important locations have additional personnel on hand to raid them after the fact."

Given that was over one hundred places, Ivy could only imagine how much man and dragon power this whole thing required.

It truly needed all the dragon clans and DDA employees from the two isles of Britain and Ireland working together to make it a reality. And according to her weekly lessons from the teachers and Zain, that wouldn't have been possible even five years ago. While enemies such as the Knights and dragon hunters had helped bring the clans together, Stonefire and Lochguard had been slowly moving relations between the clans to a more cooperative position.

Pushing aside her history lessons, she, as well as Zain, continued to stare at the speakers, neither of them wanting to miss a thing.

Dacian's voice finally returned. "The first captures are in progress. The Knights are trying to run into nearby homes in the cities, but the DDA cleared the nearby residents and stationed personnel. The runners are only going to walk into further traps." A pause, and then Dacian's voice said in a rush, "They are spreading out, running every which way. However, thanks to helicopters hovering above, we're following them closely. Oh, and now the first headquarters located in rural Wales has been raided! Snowridge is making quick work of securing prisoners and handing them over to the DDA."

Even though Ivy was in a hospital room, far from the

action, her heart thumped, her breath quickened, and she leaned forward even more. The destruction of the Dragon Knights was great for all dragon-shifters, of course, but it also meant she would no longer have a target on her back.

Excitement filled Dacian's voice as he continued, "One of the main chemical suppliers south of London has been secured. They attempted to shoot down the dragons flying overhead, but Stonefire's serum held, meaning no ill effects. And…and now part of the building exploded due to a Knight setting something off! But it seems no one on our side was injured, although Skyhunter is being more cautious as they enter the building and search out the remaining Knights inside."

While the dragons and the DDA were doing well so far, Ivy kept her ears peeled for the two biggest targets, at least in her opinion—the main research facility not far from Liverpool, England, and the other one north of Edinburgh in Scotland. The Knights could've relocated the facilities since she'd left, but if not, those two locations would have the toughest security and do-or-die protocols. Meaning the most advanced weaponry would be in those places, too.

Weapons that couldn't be stopped with any serum or other drug to protect the dragon-shifters.

Dacian's voice was even faster as he spoke again. "Clans Glenlough and Northcastle managed to surround the Knights' bases not far from the border, near Donegal in Ireland. A few of the Knights tried using a long-range flamethrower, but Glenlough's team managed to dodge and set off the aerosol sedatives before dropping them below." A few beats passed and Dacian spoke again, "All of the Knights near it are down for the count. Oh, but now Lochguard is fighting off a major laser attack at the location near Edinburgh in Scotland! One Lochguard dragon was hit, although not fatally. They're trying to regroup, but, wait, they don't need to! A team on foot was able to use tranquilizer darts to subdue them! The Scottish facility is…wait…some have entered the building, trying to save it in case anyone wants to blow it up and destroy any evidence."

Dacian paused once more, and Ivy growled. What was happening? Would they get the facility? It was one of the most important, where research she hadn't even been privy to was conducted. If the Knights managed to blow it up, so much information would be lost, information that could help the Knights reform their organization and go after the dragon-shifters again.

Zain merely rubbed her arm in calming strokes. And while he appeared not bothered, she could feel the tension of his muscles under her fingers.

Dacian finally spoke again, this time a little less hurried than before. "One of the rear buildings on the Scottish compound did explode, but Lochguard caught a handful of researchers about to set off the main building just in time. Even though it should be safe, they're quickly evacuating everyone until a more thorough sweep can be done."

Zain shared a look with her and murmured, "So hopefully, that one is saved."

"Let's hope so."

Ivy itched to get her hands on additional data and

continue her work with both the IT dragon-shifters and the doctor researchers.

Because even if they managed to destroy the vast amount of Dragon Knight strongholds, hideouts, and various facilities in the massive raid today, there would always be rogue members working alone or in small groups who would try to bring down the dragons.

While no one could help those isolated individuals filled with hatred and lies, thinking their sole purpose was to destroy dragonkind, Ivy had hope for the Knights captured during the raids. After all, Dr. Rossi had helped Ivy tremendously, and the dragonwoman had coordinated with the other dragon-shifter and human psychologists to put a large-scale exit counseling plan in place.

Dacian's voice boomed out again. "And finally, what we've all been waiting for. Stonefire launched their maneuver and are reporting the results. Nikki's wing survived intact—successfully dodging the lasers shot at them—providing the much-needed distraction for Kai's group to invade from the ground, working with Rafe and some of the British Army forces. The series of buildings disguised as a group of warehouses were all attacked at the same time. One was captured successfully, but two of the others…two of the others are threatening hostages. It seems some of the rogue dragon-shifters that had been hiding out in Scotland were captured and imprisoned by the Knights to be used for testing."

Ivy only knew the bare minimum about the so-called rogue dragon-shifters. During all the changes over the last few years in the UK, some of the clan members hadn't agreed with accepting humans onto their lands.

Over time, those dragons had trickled out or been kicked out of the various clans and had been hiding in the wild. Zain said there was more to the story, but he couldn't share the information in case someone was listening for it inside Stonefire. One minor information leak could destroy months of work the Protectors and Bram had put into place to contain those enemies, too.

Zain held Ivy a little tighter against his side, letting her know that while he cared about how all of the operations had gone, the news about Stonefire was the most important.

After all, it was his friends and colleagues risking their lives.

Dacian cheered before speaking. "The DDA came through. The mole the DDA director had placed inside the Knights' ranks months ago managed to trigger the sprinkler system for a few minutes, distracting everyone long enough for him to release the chemical into the air vents once the water turned off. That knocked everyone out."

Ivy nearly cheered herself. Bram, Kai, and Zain had taken the warning about traitors within the DDA's ranks seriously. However, they'd eventually cleared the DDA Director, Rosalind Abbott, and had conducted some secret meetings with her. Not even Ivy knew what they'd been about, but apparently, the human director had held up her end of whatever deal they'd struck.

Dacian's voice rushed out from the speakers. "Wait, they discovered one individual locked in a panic room. They're not sure if they'll be able to get him or her out for quite a while."

She shared a glance with Zain. There were tunnels under many of the most high-profile facilities, and it was entirely possible that the panic room actually had an exit somewhere.

Think of the bigger picture, Ivy. One runaway wouldn't be able to rebuild the entire organization. The worst thing that could happen was if the individual ran to the dragon hunters, hoping to find refuge.

As Dacian went on to explain all the operations had finished, and nearly all of them were successful—along with no loss of life on the dragon/DDA side but a few serious injuries—she sighed in relief. Only when Dacian signed off, saying an update would be provided later, did she finally speak to Zain again. "So, it's done, then."

He took her chin in his fingers and gently moved her head upward to better meet his gaze. "In part, thanks to you, love."

"Only a tiny bit. Most of the hard work was done by those today who risked their lives."

"But you risked yours, too, when you found your way to Stonefire."

It was hard to remember all those months ago—more than a year—when she'd constantly been looking over her shoulder as she made her way north. "Selfishly, though. I had wanted to live, and maybe wanted to get revenge for my brother, but it most definitely wasn't to help dragon-shifters for the sake of it."

He traced her bottom lip before replying, "Regardless, it took strength to make it all the way up here. I only wish I could've held up my end of the bargain when it came to finding your brother's killers specifically."

She shook her head. "Don't worry about it. At the time, that was the only connection I had left. But whilst I'll always miss my brother and David, I have a new family now. And helping and protecting them is more important than sacrificing lives to hold onto the past."

He stroked her skin, and Ivy leaned into the touch. She'd never tire of it, ever. He murmured, "I love you, Ivy Passmore. And as soon as we can get out of this bloody bed and go home again, we can start enjoying that future more."

She laughed. "I somehow see us not leaving the cottage for days after arriving, right?"

"I'd say weeks, but there's still so much for us both to do in the near future. I can't be too much of a selfish bastard and keep you all to myself."

She smiled and leaned a fraction closer, trying her best to ignore Zain's lips. "We can both be selfish for a few days, though. I think we've both earned that much, at least."

"And now my human is the randy one."

She snorted. "Nowhere near what your dragon is like, though."

As Zain's pupils flashed to slits, she didn't feel the slightest bit of fear or anxiety. Rather, the sight was comforting, a part of Zain she loved, too.

Ivy had truly reformed over the last months. And maybe, just maybe, she could help some of the others who had been like her to fully recover, too.

When Zain's pupils remained round again, he said, "I'm not even going to try to refute you, either. The bastard would make a porn star blush."

She tilted her head. "Well, then, I look forward to when we can finally kiss, and so much more."

He growled. "Don't tempt me, love. Or I'll have to leave this room to be able to restrain myself."

She clutched his top in the fingers of one hand. "No, stay. I can behave. For now."

He groaned. "You're killing me, Ivy."

She laid her head on his chest, hoping to take away the temptation to kiss her. "Only a few more days to go, Zain. Then you can do whatever you wish to me."

"I'll hold you to that, too, human."

As she snuggled against her dragonman's warm chest, Ivy sighed happily. The next few days couldn't go by fast enough.

Chapter Twenty-One

F ive days later, Zain wished Ivy would allow him to carry her to their cottage. Maybe some would say he was being immature, or insensitive, or some other bullshit, but he was anxious to claim his mate.

Today was the day Ivy had been cleared to not only go home but to kiss and do whatever came next with him.

His dragon spoke up. *The fact she can walk again, despite everything, is a massive deal to her. Let Ivy enjoy it.*

Funny you saying that, dragon, considering the accidental "nude daydreams" you've been broadcasting inside our mind.

His beast stood a little taller. *It helped me to stay calm during the operation, not killing the old dragon male who gave up Ivy's location, and the aftermath of it all.*

Right, I'm sure those are the only reasons.

His dragon grunted. *Believe what you want. But I know how much you wanted to beat that traitor to a pulp, too. My naked fantasies helped calm you down as well.*

Later, Zain had understood Kai and Bram's reasoning about Zain staying away from the old dragon male traitor. However, it'd killed him to not at least question the bastard himself.

All he knew was that the dragonman had been afraid for his children and grandchildren. Everyone had fears, but not trusting Stonefire's clan leader to handle everything was an offense itself.

He still didn't know what Bram had said to the male, but he was now serving his exile on a remote piece of land, shunned by all Stonefire.

Zain still thought prison would've been better, not caring that the dragonman was seventy-one years old.

His dragon huffed. He's under constant supervision, and even has a tracking anklet. We need to trust Bram.

I know, but it's not easy.

His dragon didn't have the chance to say anything else because Ivy emerged from her hospital room, wearing a pretty purple dress that made her eyes more indigo than blue. He walked straight up to her and placed a hand on the back of her neck, loving how her soft hair tickled the back of his hand. "Ready, love?"

The corners of her mouth ticked up. "I should be the one asking if you're ready?"

Massaging her skin, he asked, "What do you mean by that?"

She shrugged one shoulder. "I may be your true mate, I may not, but if it does prove true, then I hear your dragon becomes quite the handful."

He snorted. "Let me worry about my dragon." He moved to whisper into her ear, "Let's hurry and get you home because I'm dying to see you out of this dress."

"Zain," she said on a hitched breath.

His beast spoke up. *Imagine her saying our name repeatedly, right before she orgasms.*

Not helping, dragon.

Zain moved to stand at her side and guided her out the back entrance of the surgery.

He hadn't picked the route because he was afraid of someone attacking, but rather he suspected Daisy and Freddie were keeping an eye out for Ivy. While normally he didn't mind the pair's interest in befriending Ivy, today he wanted his human all to himself. Which meant trying to outsmart a pair of determined eleven-year-olds.

Once they hit the fresh air, Zain looked around to ensure the kids weren't lurking and then turned them toward a less-traveled path. "Come on, this way. It should be fairly deserted."

She raised a ginger eyebrow. "I thought Bram's plan going forward was to have me interact more with the clan."

"And you will, after I claim you, but not before."

"Oh."

Her breathlessness shot straight to his cock. He could just imagine her hot lips on his skin before her breath tickled and cooled his flesh.

His dragon chuckled. *Now who's the randy one?*

Ignoring his beast, he said to Ivy, "Don't worry, I'll be gentle, love. Dragons love sex, but we aren't the mindless, animalistic lot the Dragon Knights say we are."

"Of course you're not. And no, I'm not worried. If anything, I'm trying to think of anything else but what happens once we finally reach our cottage. I blush easily, and I'm trying not to be splotchy for our first time."

He smiled. "None of that matters to me, Ivy. You're the most beautiful female in the world to me."

Her cheeks turned pink, but her lips smiled wider. "Sometimes it's hard for me to reconcile this nice, romantic side of you with the first growly, rude dragonman I spotted when I woke up from my coma."

"This side of me is for you, and only you. Well, and I go soft a bit sometimes for my nephews. But no one else."

She leaned into his side. "You're good with those kids. And I think you'll make a wonderful father."

Zain missed a step but quickly righted himself. "Pardon?"

Ivy stared ahead, the wind blowing strands of her ginger hair across her face. "Seeing as I've had a lot of time confined to a bed in recent months, I've thought about what my future should look like." She met his gaze. "And even though Dr. Sid said I'm compatible with dragon-shifters and can have their children, even if I'm not a true mate, if you don't want them, that's okay. All I need is you, Zain. You are my future."

He stopped, hauled Ivy up against his front, and cupped her cheek with one hand. "I love you, Ivy Passmore, and if we have a child, I'll love them, too. But if you are all I have for the next fifty or more years, I'll be a happy male."

"Zain," she breathed.

He stroked her warm, soft cheek, wishing he could kiss her and show her just how much he wanted her. But he couldn't risk it out in the open.

So he nuzzled her other cheek and whispered, "I

know I said I'd let you walk, but I can't wait any longer, love. So I'm carrying you."

Zain scooped Ivy into his arms and ran toward their cottage. When she settled against him, looping her arms behind his neck, he knew she was just as anxious as him to claim one another.

He picked up his pace even faster, never wanting anything in his life as much as he wanted to claim the female in his arms.

SNUGGLED IN ZAIN'S ARMS, Ivy listened to his breathing and heartbeat as their cottage came into view.

Even though she'd done a pretty good job of not blushing—or, at least she thought so—her heart thumped so fast she didn't know how every dragon-shifter in a mile radius couldn't hear it.

After all the days, weeks, and months of recovery and restraint, she was finally going to have sex with her dragonman.

And even if their conversation about children hadn't been clear, he at least knew how she felt. Because it was true—Zain was her future. Without him forcing his way into her life, she didn't know what would've become of her.

Because while it sounded corny, sometimes it did take love to truly help a person change for the better.

Zain finally reached their front door and stopped to put his ear to it. She whispered, "What are you doing?"

A few beats passed before he sighed in relief. "No

one's in there. I just wanted to make sure Freddie and Daisy aren't inside waiting with another surprise party."

She smiled. "Don't worry, I asked Dawn and Sasha to keep them busy this afternoon."

"Just *this* afternoon?" he growled.

Ivy resisted laughing at Zain's tone. "Well, for the foreseeable future, at any rate. Although I did promise we'd host a game night for them in the near future, so you'd better be up for it."

"Fine, fine, as long as they stay away for at least a week, I'd be willing to carry them up into the air in my dragon form."

As he opened the door, she snorted. "I wouldn't tempt fate. I'm sure Daisy is already planning on how to accomplish that."

He shut the door with his foot. "I don't care about Daisy right now."

She caught his heated gaze before Zain ascended the stairs, her heart pumping with each step.

This was it. She was finally going to be claimed by her dragonman.

Ivy only hoped she lived up to the expectation. Anticipation could make things sweeter, but it could also lead to greater disappointment.

Zain abruptly dumped her on the bed and leaned back. As his gaze raked over her—his pupils flashing—he ordered, "Strip for me."

For a second, she hesitated. However, as Zain continued to stare at her as if she were a choice piece of meat he was ready to devour, her nerves eased. He wanted her as she was, and he'd never show disappointment at how she was still too thin, or how many freckles she had.

So Ivy slipped a strap of her dress off one shoulder, and then the other, holding the front against her chest to keep it from falling to her waist.

Zain growled and took a step forward. "Do I need to rip it off myself? I've waited a long time to see your gorgeous body, love. I don't want to wait anymore."

She shook her head with a smile, a small thrill going up her spine at how he thought her gorgeous. His words boosted her confidence, so she said, "Not yet. After all this time, another minute won't kill you."

"It might," he muttered, but stayed in place.

Ivy rested on her knees and inched the dress down, never taking her gaze from Zain's face. His pupils flashed faster with each inch of exposed skin, and when she finally let the top section drop, revealing her naked to the waist, he moved a hand to the front of his jeans and adjusted the hard bulge in his crotch.

Even though it had been years since the last time she'd seen a naked, aroused man, she imagined Zain's cock out in front of him, glistening at the tip for her.

Heat surged through her body, straight between her thighs, ending at the pounding ache there.

She'd teased him about being impatient, but Ivy was just as much so.

Wanting him naked and inside her, Ivy shimmied out of the rest of her dress until she sat naked on the bed. She'd wondered about her decision not to wear underwear leaving the surgery, but as Zain's gaze darted to her patch of reddish curls and growled, she decided she liked expediency. "Take off your clothes and claim me, Zain." She moved to lay on her back, resting her arms above her head, her legs spread wide. "I'm waiting."

He quickly tore off his clothes with a growl and was above her on his hands and knees in less than a minute.

Maybe if his hard dick wasn't brushing her belly right this second, she'd ask him to back up a bit so she could see his naked body properly.

However, the hot hardness pressing against her only made the pounding between her legs intensify. She could see him later. After all, they had the rest of their lives together.

So Ivy arched her hips, wanting, no needing, to have him inside her. "Why are you merely hovering above me still?"

His voice was husky as he answered, "I don't know if there'll be a frenzy or not, so I'm trying to remember you right now, laying on the bed naked, waiting for me just in case instinct takes over. Because I won't be able to stop and simply admire you until it's complete, love. I hope you know that."

Raising a hand, she placed it on the back of his neck. "Kiss me, Zain. I don't care if there's a frenzy or not. I just want my mate to claim me."

He took a deep breath before saying, "If there's a frenzy, there will be a child."

"I know. And either way, whether it happens or not, if you are willing to take the risk, then so am I."

Zain slowly lowered his body onto hers, and Ivy moaned at his hard, warm skin against hers. And when his cock brushed her clit, she gasped.

He nuzzled one cheek, and then the other, the light brush of scruff only making her hotter. He finally hovered an inch from her lips and murmured, "It's time to finally claim my mate. You're mine, Ivy. And only mine."

"Yes, yours. So kiss me already."

As soon as her lips touched his, Ivy opened her mouth and moaned as he licked, nibbled, and explored every inch. She had no idea if her kiss had kicked off anything, but she didn't care. She was too busy kissing him back, letting him know she wanted him as much as he wanted her.

ZAIN HAD NEARLY DRAWN blood by digging his nails into his palms as Ivy had slowly undressed. He'd never thought that someone merely taking off clothes could be sexy as hell, but he'd never been so hard in his life as his little mate had done it.

And when she'd exposed her small breasts, he itched to suckle one of her nipples until she screamed. So he'd only dug his nails in harder to stop himself.

His dragon spoke up. *Why hold back? We've waited long enough.*

I don't want to scare her.

She won't be. Ivy trusts us.

However, before he could reply, Ivy removed her dress and lay back on the bed. As she spread her legs wide, he could see her glistening already.

And yet, despite his pulsing cock, he stayed in place.

He'd let Ivy call the shots the first time, just in case there was a frenzy.

And even if there wasn't, Zain wasn't sure he could remain gentle and patient as the night wore on. His dragon would want to come out at some point, and they possessed the more animalistic side of their bed play.

I could behave, his beast grumbled.

However, the second Ivy said, "I'm waiting," he ignored his dragon and ripped off his clothes with his talons and moved to hover above her on his hands and knees. When the head of his cock brushed her belly, he hissed, and his dick let out a drop of precum.

Fuck, he wanted to spread her wide and show her just how much he wanted her.

But she needed to be prepared. So somehow, he managed to warn her about frenzies and pregnancies, but Ivy didn't worry about either.

By the time he nuzzled one of her cheeks and then the other, his balls were so tight he didn't think he'd last long once he was finally inside his mate.

Which was unacceptable.

So he took a deep breath to calm his cock a fraction and then finally lowered his lips to hers and kissed her.

There was no jolt of need or desire to fuck her until she was pregnant. And maybe at some point, he'd have cared about her being his true mate or not. However, Zain barely paid it any attention, loving how fucking incredible she tasted—better than he could've ever imagined.

He explored her mouth with his tongue, licking, stroking, showing her how much he needed her.

And when Ivy tangled back with his tongue, he groaned and took the kiss deeper as he moved a hand down to one of her nipples. He plucked and lightly squeezed the tight bud, and Ivy cried out.

But he never ceased his attention to either her mouth or her breasts.

His dragon hummed. *More, taste more of her. Let her know how much we treasure her, or I will take control.*

Even though he'd later let his dragon do so—they were one and the same, and he'd never deny his beast—he wasn't about to surrender his first time.

So Zain moved his hand from her breasts down her body until he reached between her thighs. He groaned at how wet she was. "I can take it slow later, but I need to claim you, Ivy, and fast."

It was hard to concentrate on her words with her swollen lips and flushed cheeks, but somehow he managed. "Is it the frenzy?"

"No, but that doesn't mean I want you any less."

Her hand ran down his back, to his arse, and she lightly dug her nails in. "Then take me, dragonman. I think we've both waited long enough."

His dragon cheered as Zain leaned back and spread her legs wider. He wasn't going to be as thorough as he wanted this first time, but he still took a second to lightly run his finger through her center and then bring his finger to his mouth. He licked her sweet honey and moaned. "Maybe I should try to hold on as I need much more than one taste of you."

Ivy bent her legs and arched her hips. "Zain, please.

Don't make either of us wait any longer. I want you inside me, dragonman. Now."

At the wanting and commanding of her tone, all other thoughts vanished but pleasing his mate. He positioned his cock at her entrance and ran the head back and forth, loving how she squirmed in the process. Only when he was sure she was wet enough did he gently push forward. He groaned. "Fuck, Ivy, you're so tight."

He moved a few more inches, the way she gripped him, combined with her hotness, was nearly too much.

Zain gritted his teeth and finally thrust in to the hilt. Ivy arched her back and moaned.

Needing to taste something of her, he leaned down and took her lips. She instantly grabbed his biceps and started kissing him back.

Unable to restrain himself any longer, he rolled his hips, increasing his pace each time. Ivy hitched her feet behind his back and soon joined him in the rhythm, moving as if nothing else mattered but him claiming her.

Somewhere in the back of his mind, Zain knew he needed to do more for Ivy. Since she wasn't his true mate, his semen wouldn't make her orgasm, which meant he needed to ensure it happened each and every time he claimed her. That's what every mate deserved.

He moved a hand to her clit and lightly stroked as he thrust.

She broke the kiss and cried out. "Faster, Zain. Right there, but faster."

He didn't hold back, taking her over and over again until all he could hear was their harsh breaths and the sound of flesh slapping against flesh.

The pressure building at the base of his spine told him he needed to focus more on Ivy, or he'd come first.

And his mate should always orgasm first.

So Zain pressed a little firmer against her hard bud, loving how she squeezed his cock in response.

It seemed his mate liked it fast and hard.

"Mm, Zain. So, so close."

Hoping to push her over the edge, he pinched her clit, and Ivy screamed as her pussy pulsed around him.

Despite how incredible it felt, making him want to join her, Zain continued to thrust and hold back, wanting her to finish first.

When she finally relaxed against the bed, he thrust one, two, three more times and then stilled with a roar. As he came inside her, Ivy screamed out again in pleasure, her pussy relentlessly milking him for every last drop.

Once they both finally came down from their highs, Zain collapsed next to Ivy and pulled her tight against his chest. It took her a second to catch her breath, but she finally said, "I don't know how you managed it, but that was amazing, Zain."

He kissed her forehead and reveled in her scent. "You've ruined me for all other females, love."

"I hope so. Because I'm not sharing."

He chuckled and hugged her closer. As they enjoyed the comfortable silence, his dragon spoke up. *Something was strange.*

What was strange?

She orgasmed when we came. Only true mates react to semen that way.

Zain's brain wasn't firing on all cylinders so soon after sex, so he took a second to think about his dragon's words.

It was true. Only a dragon's true mate orgasmed at that moment.

Which meant that prior to her treatment, Ivy had been his. Even though his dragon didn't have the overwhelming need to impregnate her, she still reacted to him.

He must've said something aloud because Ivy asked, "What's wrong?"

His dragon said, *Just tell her.*

Looking down to meet Ivy's eyes, he explained what had happened and added, "That's going to be a regular thing for you, love, so you'd better get used to it."

She beamed up at him. "I think I can handle that. But it's also interesting, don't you think?"

He sighed. "I can barely think right now after the way your pussy clenched my cock, love. So just tell me."

"Well, in the end, even a former Dragon Knight and dragon-shifter can be perfect for each other."

He kissed her gently before replying, "I suppose so, although it took a little persuading on both sides. It's you who won me over, Ivy Passmore. Not fate."

Mischief danced in her eyes. "Maybe I need a tad more persuading, then, to make doubly sure we're perfect together. Maybe four or more orgasms? Then I can agree with you and accept fate."

With a growl, he rolled until she was on her back. He moved his face until it was an inch from hers. "Right, then I'm going to make them unforgettable, so as to not leave any doubts." He lowered his voice, fully aware his pupils had to be flashing. "And we're going to start with the first two only coming from my tongue."

As he moved down her body to do exactly that, Zain couldn't help but smile. Fate had somehow been right, but just because that was true didn't mean he'd ever take his female for granted.

Epilogue

Years Later

Ivy signed off her latest video call, leaned back in her office chair, and placed a hand over her swollen belly. She murmured to her unborn child, "It seems Matilda has fallen for a dragonman as well. I'm glad."

Matilda was one of the numerous former Dragon Knights Ivy had worked with over the years, doing what she could to help them shed the lies and misconceptions that had been ingrained into them by the Knights.

While not everyone had been savable—or even had wanted to try—Ivy continued to follow up with all those who had.

Because every time someone like Matilda found happiness with what had once been a former enemy, it made her smile brighter.

Glancing at the time, she sighed. Even though Freddie and Daisy were teenagers now, they still demanded game nights at least once a month. And not even Ivy being heavily pregnant would stop them. If she were in labor, Daisy might still try to get a quick game going.

Chuckling to herself, Ivy managed to finally heft herself out of the chair and head toward the door. As soon as she opened it, she found Zain standing outside it. "How long have you been there?"

"Too long. You should've been done half an hour ago, love."

As Zain pulled her against his chest—she had to partially turn these days because of her pregnancy—she snuggled into his heat and said, "Matilda had some big news—she's going to mate one of the dragon-shifters on Skyhunter. I couldn't very well say, 'Sorry, time's up! Have a good time,' now, could I?"

He grunted. "I would have."

She laughed. "You would think after years of being mated, you might occasionally want some time away."

"Never." He cupped her cheek. "Besides, it's not just me. You know Daisy will coordinate a search party, even if it means risking Tristan and Bram's ire."

"Speaking of which, if we don't put the pizza in the oven, it won't be ready in time. And I don't know about you, but I don't want teenagers already raging with hormones to also be starving."

He kissed her gently before turning her to be at his side. "I think from now on, we should stipulate that they do the cooking for these blasted things. I won't have you overtiring yourself once the baby comes."

She placed a hand on her stomach and rubbed

lightly. "If I wear myself out placing a pizza in an oven and setting the timer, then I have bigger things to worry about."

Zain growled, but she reached over and placed his hand on the other side of her stomach. As happened often, the little one kicked at Zain's presence. Her mate's expression softened. Ivy continued, "I think you're just anxious to meet this one, and I think it'll be great to have their cousins around as he or she grows up."

In times like these, Ivy often thought of the family her child would never meet—her brother and his partner. But all she could do was tell her child some wonderful stories of the uncles they'd never meet.

Zain kissed her cheek, bringing her back to the present. He replied, "As long as they don't start teaching our little one how to get into trouble from the day they start walking, then maybe it would be nice to have them around."

She bit her lip to keep from smiling. Ivy had long ago learned that Zain tried to be tough, even when he didn't need to be. Rarely so with her anymore, but she thought he might try to do it for their child.

Since she still had over a month to talk to him about it, she motioned her head toward the kitchen. "Come on, or we'll have some grumpy teenagers soon enough."

As she leaned against her mate and they walked down the hallway together, her baby did a somersault inside her belly, making her smile wider.

It was hard to believe at one time she had hated so unconditionally. But thankfully, she'd found her perfect match and now only had a life overflowing with love.

Author's Note

A huge thanks to my readers for their patience with this story. I effectively took a two-year break from my Stone-fire series to write about other dragon-shifter clans (Lochguard, Skyhunter, Snowridge, and even PineRock). While I know some people probably gave up on me for that, all of the UK-based books I wrote play into what happened in *Persuading the Dragon*. This book took a huge step forward in the overall universe storyline. And to make it all believable, a lot of little things needed to be put into place.

Also, writing a true enemies-to-lovers story is difficult because the pacing is so important. It's not hyperbole to say this is one of the hardest books I've written in a while. But with it done, I can have a little more fun before we have to deal with the dragon hunters, too.

As always, there are some people I'd like to thank for their help:

• Becky Johnson and her team at Hot Tree Editing. Becky always catches the little things, and even after all these years, she still makes me a better writer.

• Iliana G., Donna H., Sabrina D., and Sandy H. are my fantastic beta-readers and they catch the lingering typos and inconsistencies. Iliana in particular pointed out a scientific uh-oh I missed, which I then fixed! Thanks to all my wonderful betas.

And lastly, thanks to you, the reader. You make my dream job a reality! At the time of writing this, we're coming up on the Six Year Anniversary of *Sacrificed to the Dragon*, which started this crazy journey. Here's to hoping you follow along for many more books to come. I'll see you at the end of the next story! Turn the page for glimpses of some of my other books.

The Dragon's Choice

TAHOE DRAGON MATES #1

After Jose Santos's younger sister secretly enters them both into the yearly dragon lottery and they get selected, he begrudgingly agrees to participate. It means picking a human female from a giant room full of them and staying around just long enough to get her pregnant. However, when his dragon notices one female who keeps hiding behind a book, Jose has a new plan—win his fated mate, no matter what it takes.

Victoria Lewis prefers being home with a book and away from large crowds. But she desperately wants to study dragon-shifters at close range, so she musters up her courage to enter the dragon lottery. When she's selected as one of the potential candidates, she decides to accept her spot. After all, it's not as if the dragon-shifter will pick her—an introverted bookworm who prefers jeans and sweats to skirts or fancy clothes. Well, until he's standing right in front of her with flashing eyes and says he wants her.

As Jose tries to win his fated female, trouble stirs inside his clan. Will he be able to keep his mate with him forever? Or will the American Department of Dragon Affairs whisk her away to some other clan to protect her?

NOTE: This is a quick, steamy standalone story about fated mates and sexy dragon-shifters near Lake Tahoe in the USA. You don't have to read all my other dragon books to enjoy this one!

The Dragon's Choice is available in paperback.

Treasured by the Dragon

STONEFIRE DRAGONS #13

If someone had told Dawn Chadwick that she'd be attending a play put on by children on a dragon-shifter's land a year ago, she would've said they were mad. However, her daughter Daisy has slowly worn Dawn down about her prejudices and she ends up volunteering to help with the play. She's to assist an eccentric drag-onman with the special effects. What she didn't count on was her daughter's meddling.

Blake Whitby prefers working in a lab to being around people. He's a rare white dragon with a black spot, and the attention from a young age has made him hide from others. However, he's always had a weakness for children and agrees to help them with their play. What he didn't count on was meeting a beautiful human with a sense of humor and a heart-warming smile. His dragon wants her, but Blake holds back. At least until two kids make holding back impossible.

While Dawn agrees to the mate-claim frenzy with Blake, there's no guarantee their pairing will work. And when Dawn's family threatens to cut her and Daisy off, Blake has to convince them both he wants them as his future.

Treasured by the Dragon will be available in paperback Fall 2020.

Also by Jessie Donovan

Asylums for Magical Threats

Blaze of Secrets (AMT #1)

Frozen Desires (AMT #2)

Shadow of Temptation (AMT #3)

Flare of Promise (AMT #4)

Cascade Shifters

Convincing the Cougar (CS #0.5)

Reclaiming the Wolf (CS #1)

Cougar's First Christmas (CS #2)

Resisting the Cougar (CS #3)

Kelderan Runic Warriors

The Conquest (KRW #1)

The Barren (KRW #2)

The Heir (KRW #3)

The Forbidden (KRW #4)

The Hidden (KRW #5)

The Survivor / Kajala Mayven (KRW #6 / TBD)

Lochguard Highland Dragons

The Dragon's Dilemma (LHD #1)

Treasured by the Dragon / Dawn and Blake (SD #13 / Sept 2020)

Stonefire Dragons Shorts

Meeting the Humans (SDS #1)

The Dragon Camp (SDS #2)

The Dragon Play (SDS #3)

Stonefire Dragons Universe

Winning Skyhunter (SDU #1)

Transforming Snowridge (SDU #2)

Tahoe Dragon Mates

The Dragon's Choice (TDM #1)

The Dragon's Need (TDM #2)

The Dragon's Bidder (TDM #3 / July 2020)

WRITING AS LIZZIE ENGLAND

Her Fantasy

Holt: The CEO

Callan: The Highlander

Adam: The Duke

Gabe: The Rock Star

About the Author

Jessie Donovan has sold over half a million books, has given away hundreds of thousands more to readers for free, and has even hit the *NY Times* and *USA Today* bestseller lists. She is best known for her dragon-shifter series, but also writes about elemental magic users, alien warriors, and even has a crazy romantic comedy series set in Scotland. When not reading a book, attempting to tame her yard, or traipsing around some foreign country on a shoestring, she can often be found interacting with her readers on Facebook. She lives near Seattle, where, yes, it rains a lot but it also makes everything green.

Visit her website at: www.JessieDonovan.com

Printed in Poland
by Amazon Fulfillment
Poland Sp. z o.o., Wrocław

58795034R00162